"Tell you what

"Let's just take this one day at a time. No rules or expectations. Just fun."

"Yeah," said Rose, blindsiding him with a smile that didn't quite reach her eyes. She was such a contradiction. All at once full of life, and yet heartbreaking in her buried sorrow. With everything in him, he wanted to be everything to her. But even he was smart enough to realize he didn't have that kind of power. "Let's just play."

"Walk me out?"

"Mmm-hmm."

Offering his hand to help her from the sofa, Dalton took the short trek to the back door with her in companionable silence. He kissed her forehead. She gave his waist a squeeze, and he left, knowing that no matter what else happened between them, his life was forever, irrevocably changed by Rose Vasquez's smile.

Dear Reader,

Ahh… Don't you just love dancing? Er, I mean watching *other* people dance. For years, hubby and I have been talking about taking a ballroom dancing class. But then, we've also been talking about going on a diet, and that hasn't happened, either!

Anyway, I just adore all the gliding and dipping and long, lusty looks that go along with formal dances. As a little girl, I took tap dancing for a few weeks, but never quite got the hang of it. From there I progressed to ballet, but my first tutu wedgie pretty much put the kibosh on what I'm sure would otherwise have been a stellar career!

Seeing how I must have four of those proverbial left feet, I decided to work out my dancing frustrations on poor Dalton and Rose. Now, Rose is a pro, but Dalton would rather dig ditches than set foot in a dance studio. Lucky for him Rose's sultry good looks and amazing talent actually make learning the tango fun! But will it also help him fill the emptiness in his heart? I'm not telling. Turn the page to find out!

Happy reading!

Laura Marie

DANCING WITH DALTON
Laura Marie Altom

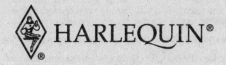

HARLEQUIN®

TORONTO • NEW YORK • LONDON
AMSTERDAM • PARIS • SYDNEY • HAMBURG
STOCKHOLM • ATHENS • TOKYO • MILAN • MADRID
PRAGUE • WARSAW • BUDAPEST • AUCKLAND

ISBN-13: 978-0-373-75182-2
ISBN-10:   0-373-75182-6

DANCING WITH DALTON

www.eHarlequin.com

Printed in U.S.A.

ABOUT THE AUTHOR

After college (Go Hogs!), bestselling, award-winning author Laura Marie Altom did a brief stint as an interior designer before becoming a stay-at-home mom to boy/girl twins. Always an avid romance reader, she knew it was time to try her hand at writing when she found herself replotting the afternoon soaps.

When not immersed in her next story, Laura enjoys an almost glamorous lifestyle of zipping around in a convertible while trying to keep her dog from leaping out, and constantly striving to reach the bottom of the laundry basket—a feat she may never accomplish! For real fun, Laura is content to read, do needlepoint and cuddle with her kids and handsome hubby.

Laura loves hearing from readers at either P.O. Box 2074, Tulsa, OK 74101, or e-mail: BaliPalm@aol.com. Love lounging on the beach while winning fun stuff? Check out lauramariealtom.com!

Books by Laura Marie Altom

For the newest member of our family, Russell Shook.
I love you, sweetie!

Chapter One

"Next on the agenda," Alice Craigmoore said in her raspy, Southern drawl, "is this year's Miss Hot Pepper pageant. Mona, as our reigning pageant chair, do you have a report?"

Dalton Montgomery took this as his cue to commence with a nap.

The private back room of Duffy's Barbecue was famous for not only its fishing-themed decor, but also its oak and leather chairs roomy enough to allow a guy to enjoy a man-size meal without feeling sliced in half. In other words, it was easy to tune out of the bimonthly meeting's most mind-numbing portions.

As president-elect of Hot Pepper, Louisiana's chamber of commerce, Dalton had no problem tackling ordinary business matters. But whenever his fellow members started in with one of their half-dozen festivals they'd planned, or God forbid this pageant, he felt completely out of his league. But then these days, was there anywhere he did feel comfortable and in control?

As the only son of the president of the First National Bank of Hot Pepper, Dalton had been expected since birth to one day step into his father's shoes. The one time he'd deviated from the plan, he'd failed miserably both personally and professionally, leading him to believe maybe fate was smarter than he was.

Fifteen years later, here he was, resigned to living the rest of his days in a twelve-by-twelve office with an alley view.

Rubbing his forehead, he stifled a groan.

He wasn't usually so cranky about his lot in life. He had a large group of family and friends. A great house. Pool. Shiny new red Escalade. In the grand scheme of things, he didn't have much to complain about.

So why was it that when he'd shaved this morning, the guy gazing back at him in the mirror had looked damn near dead?

"Dalton?" Mona asked. "Haven't you heard a word of what I've just said?"

"Huh?" He glanced up.

All ten chamber of commerce members present stared his way.

"The outgoing Miss Hot Pepper. It's your responsibility to tango with her during the lag time when the judges tally their scores."

Nope. Not going to happen. "I thought it was the president's responsibility to do the whole cheesy dance thing?"

"Cheesy?" Alice and Mona said in equally outraged tones.

"I'll have you know," Mona said, "that the end-of-pageant dance is a tradition that's been alive longer than you."

"And as incoming president," Alice piped in, "seeing how you're a man, you'll have to perform. After all, you wouldn't want to see me up there dancing with the beauty queen, would you?"

Hell, no. But that didn't mean he wanted to do it, either. "Why does it have to be me? There are twenty other guys I'm sure would be thrilled for the opportunity. For that matter, doesn't the outgoing Miss Hot Pepper have a boyfriend? Why can't you use him?"

"It's not that bad," Frank Loveaux said, loosening his brown striped tie. The man had a triple chin, so Dalton could see where the business noose would hinder his breathing. "I did it three years ago and had a ball. That was back when Mindy Sue Jacobs was Miss Hot Pepper." He whistled, then grinned. "That little lady was a pistol. To this day, I still dream about the kiss she gave me at the end of our dance."

"That's all well and good," Dalton said, "but everyone knows I can't dance. Just ask my prom date—over a decade later, and she's still crippled from my stepping on her toes."

"My daughter's toes work just fine," Catherine Bennett—mother of his prom date, Josie—said. "Why are you being so obstinate? If it weren't for your arguing, we could've been three more items down the agenda."

Ouch. He and Josie hadn't lasted much beyond prom.

Her eagle-eyed, blunt-talking mother had been a huge part of the problem. That, and the fact that Josie had been pretty and sweet and all, but she hadn't lit any fires in his belly. His mama had always told him that if a girl didn't keep him awake at night, craving their next kiss, it was time to move on.

Well, here he was, thirty-five years old, and aside from his ex, Carly, sleeping like a rock. Not that he lacked for female companionship. Just that to date, no woman except Carly had come anywhere near making him feel alive. *Complete.* But she had changed all that by slashing his heart in a zillion pieces. Now he vastly preferred the single life. He might occasionally be lonely, but the alternative of being emotionally annihilated sucked.

Alice slammed her gavel against the speaker's podium. "I'd like to make a motion that Dalton perform the end-of-pageant tango. All in favor?"

Nine arms shot up. "Aye."

"Opposed?"

"Nay," Dalton alone said.

With another slam of her gavel, his fate was sealed. "The ayes have it. Next on the agenda—the Hot Pepper Festival's food concessions. Frank, are you ready with your report?"

WHOA.

Dalton's first glimpse of the hottie greeting him in the dance studio's pale pink reception area had him doing a double take. "Um, you're not blue-haired Miss Gertrude."

Flashing a professional smile that didn't reach her eyes, the vision said, "Miss Gertrude retired. I'm the studio's new owner, Rose Vasquez. Are you the Dalton Montgomery I have down for a tango lesson?"

"That'd be me," he said. For the first time since that week's chamber meeting, he stopped cursing his fellow committee members. Maybe the whole dance gig wouldn't be half-bad.

"Welcome." She held out her slim hand for him to shake.

When their palms met, he felt a twinge in his gut. Her grip was firm, yet somehow fragile, as if the merest hint of a wind might blow her away. Aside from a trickling lobby fountain and humming drink machine, the studio was quiet—save for his racing pulse. He hadn't expected them to be alone. Not that it was a problem. Just that, being in a small-town dance studio, he'd pictured himself surrounded by eight-year-old gigglers in pink tutus.

Clasping her hands over her gently curved belly, she said, "The woman who made your reservation—"

"My secretary—Joan."

"Yes, well, Joan, mentioned you just need a *crash* course."

"Yep. That'll do it. The basics are all I need to get me through one heinous night."

"That's all well and good," the woman said, her once lovely expression now sober, "but when you say you want to know *just the basics* about the tango, you've insulted not only me, but a tradition that has lasted more than a hundred years. Tango isn't *just* a dance, and I hope that once we're finished with our lessons, you'll see that. I also hope you'll treat this venture we're embarking upon with the dignity and respect it deserves—even loyalty."

Dignity and respect? Loyalty? Dalton figured he deserved an Academy Award—at least an Emmy—for the acting job he was doing in holding back a snort. They were talking about dance moves. This woman might be attractive, but she had a lot to learn about what in life deserved such sentiments. If anyone was an expert on what loyalty made a man do, it was him.

"You're awfully quiet," she said, tapping a purple pencil against the top of a yellow laminate reception desk. The girlie colors brought on indigestion, or was it the fact that he was for all practical purposes being lectured by a stranger that had his stomach in an uproar?

He reached into the chest pocket of his suit for a chewable antacid, but he was fresh out. Damn.

When he spotted her eyeing him funny, he withdrew his hand from his pocket. "I'm assuming from the tone of our one-sided conversation that either I play this dancing game all your way or hit the highway?"

She smiled, and the force of it nearly knocked him off his feet. She wasn't merely hot, as he'd previously thought. She was beautiful. In fact, she could've launched an entire new category of beauty. Rich, olive-toned skin served as the perfect backdrop for soulful brown eyes and silky, raven-black hair that his finger-tips itched to touch.

Snap out of it! his conscience cried.

She was a looker, but considering the tone of the speech she'd just delivered, she was also a few cupcakes shy of a dozen.

Smile not reaching her eyes, she said, "I can't say anyone has ever paraphrased my wishes so eloquently, but yes, you're right. If I agree to give you a crash course in tango, you must give me as close to one hundred percent of yourself as possible."

When he opened his mouth to object, she shocked him by placing the pad of her index finger against his lips.

"No," she said, "don't speak. I can read your mind. You're thinking how can you devote all your energy to learning this dance when work is what you live for, am I right?"

He nodded.

"As you'll soon see, I'm not asking for much. Just your undivided attention."

Right. From where he stood, sounded more like his soul.

"Do we have a deal, Mr. Montgomery?"

Telling himself he felt the same jolt of awareness every time he shook a female colleague's hand, Dalton once again grasped the lovely Ms. Vasquez's fingers in his. "Deal. Ready to start?"

"You mean now?"

"My secretary did make a reservation."

"No," she said with a faint shake of her head. "I—I'm sorry, but something has come up. I have lessons from noon until six tomorrow evening. You and I shall tango at seven."

AFTER MR. MONTGOMERY left, Rose had trouble locking the door. Her fingers trembled as she remembered the spark of interest in Dalton Montgomery's striking blue eyes. Her stomach clenched when she considered how close she'd come to reaching out to straighten a wayward lock of his unruly short, dark hair. At just over six feet, with a square jaw, high brow and Roman nose, Dalton exuded strength and undeniable sex appeal.

Why had she lectured him like that? Why had she turned away the good money she could've earned from tonight's session?

The truth?

Not because she was eager to check on Anna as she'd told herself, but because for the first time since John's death well over a year earlier, she'd found a man attractive, and the notion shook her to the core.

The thought of spending an hour in Dalton Montgomery's arms while performing the dance she'd so loved with her husband, well… It was inconceivable. Which was why she'd bought herself a little extra time. To adjust to the idea that it was okay to find another man physically attractive.

Find him attractive yes, but feel warmth spreading through her limbs when he looked at her? What had that been about? How could she begin to process her mixed-up feelings in the all-too-brief time until they met again?

Somehow, some way, she'd found the strength to tackle each day since the motorcycle accident that'd stolen John from her and Anna. Rose forced a deep breath, knowing she'd capably handle this development, as well.

In the brief time they'd shared as man and wife, she and her husband had enjoyed a wholly fulfilling physical relationship. She'd always been a passionate woman. It was common sense that as a healthy female in her prime she would have certain needs. Logically, the attraction she'd felt for Mr. Montgomery had been purely biological—nothing at all to be concerned about.

Oh yeah? Then how come your pulse is racing at the mere thought of seeing him again?

She didn't have an answer—at least one she was willing to admit, even to herself. Rose flicked off the studio's lights then resolutely marched up the stairs to her and Anna's airy loft.

In coming to terms with John's death, Anna had been her rock. Tonight, whether the six-year-old knew it or not, she would again be her mom's strength.

As for Dalton Montgomery, all Rose had to do to deal with him was convince herself that he was just another student and the tango was just another dance.

EARLY THURSDAY evening, an hour before her lesson with Mr. Montgomery, Rose trudged up the stairs.

Since crawling out of bed that morning, dread had

settled low in her stomach. Now, entering the high-ceilinged kitchen she thought of as her private sanctuary, she didn't bother masking full-on panic. Luckily, Anna was out for dinner and a movie with a friend.

Though Rose wasn't hungry, it'd been noon since she'd last eaten, so she slipped off her heels, then prepared a light meal of tomato soup.

While waiting for the creamy liquid to boil, she gazed about the massive space, loving the slant of late-spring sun through the towering bank of west windows.

She adored plants and the brightness of the place—not to mention the high ceilings and lack of interior walls—allowed her to house a collection of trees. Palms, miniature oranges and even a red maple she'd been given as a housewarming gift but hadn't quite gotten around to planting in the historic brick building's postage stamp of a backyard. Her know-it-all brothers had assured her that the tree would die after being inside over a week, but months later, it still thrived.

Giving the soup a stir, she mused that a lot of people—especially her overprotective father and two big brothers—had thought her business would die. But it'd been ninety days since she'd opened her doors and while she wouldn't say her business was thriving, it was holding its own. Just like her and Anna.

Together, they were learning to weather grief, life's toughest storm.

What about the storm you're about to face in partnering with Dalton Montgomery?

A burning, sweet scent filled her nostrils a second before the telltale sizzle of liquid hit the gas burner's flame.

Rats. In all her daydreaming, she'd forgotten her soup. She twisted off the heat and cleaned the oozing red mess. So much for supper.

Grabbing saltines from the pantry, she plopped into her favorite overstuffed armchair. She knew it'd sound silly to anyone else, but the chair had been John's, and sitting in it was akin to getting a hug. At times, she'd have sworn she still smelled his citrus aftershave on the brown leather.

She switched on the local news, but when the bulk of the broadcast consisted of an extended sports segment, she turned it off, and her eyes drifted shut....

"Ahem. Ms. Vasquez?"

Rose jerked to attention only to find Dalton Montgomery standing less than twelve inches away!

"Sorry," Mr. Montgomery said. "I didn't mean to startle you."

Rose scooted to an upright position and tried to quickly pull herself together. Her hair was probably a mess and she did her best to shove it back into a metal clip.

"Don't," her uninvited guest said, eyeing her in his annoyingly direct way.

"Don't what?"

"Fix your hair. It looks...fine. Like that." He swallowed hard. "Down." *Wild.* While he hadn't voiced that last part, she sensed that was what he'd meant. Which was why she went ahead with the task of smoothing her hair back and purposefully snapping the clip.

His tone made her do a quick check to ensure her nap hadn't resulted in a wardrobe malfunction. Nope, all was well with her formfitting black dress. It was her mind that seemed in trouble. What was it about him that left her off balance?

"Why are you here?" she asked, adopting the coldly professional tone she used with unruly junior-high students forced to take waltz classes by their parents.

"I have a lesson. Remember?" He tapped his watch. "It's already seven-fifteen. I smelled something burning and worried there was a problem, especially seeing how all the doors were unlocked but no one was there."

"So you barged into my home?"

"Whoa. Look, lady, I don't know what you're so defensive about all of a sudden, but I was only trying to be a Good Samaritan. Your door was wide open. I thought your place might be on fire. I came in to make sure you were okay. End of story. Now, are we going to dance, or what?"

Or what? Good question.

As was the matter of why she was so snippy.

She rarely slept through the night, which left her napping during the day. Usually to be poked awake by her assistant, Rachel—currently on maternity leave. Which was why she'd left the door open out of habit. Mr. Montgomery's explanation had been plausible. Even admirable. His small-town brand of ingrained, instantaneous caring was a large part of the reason she'd packed up Anna and made the move from their impersonal Dallas high-rise to the town of Hot Pepper. She'd moved because she wanted to raise her daughter in a place populated with friendly folks. Double-checking her barrette, Rose stood. "I'm the one who should be sorry. With prom season right around the corner, I've been giving more private lessons than usual. All the overtime has me not quite myself."

"It's okay. When under pressure, I tend to go all grizzly on folks, too." A quirky bear growl escaped his lips as he held up his fingers, feigning ferocious claws.

"Do you?" she asked, for whatever strange reason needing to know that he did truly understand.

He answered with a sad laugh as his lips fell into an unmistakable frown. They were firm lips. Yet soft. Intriguing, as if he held the power to kiss a woman senseless... Assuming she wanted to be kissed. Which she didn't. Just that—

"Yes, Ms. Vasquez, I understand more than you could possibly know on the subject of how too much work affects people." With a light sigh, he gestured to the floral-print sofa. "Mind if I have a seat?"

"Of course not. Please..." She gestured for him to make himself comfortable.

Dressed as he was in loose-fitting faded jeans and a chest-hugging orange-and-black Princeton T-shirt, he was a different man from the suit she'd met the previous night.

"Whew," he said. "It feels good taking a load off.

Down at the bank I've been pacing my office floor. A company my investment group is interested in acquiring tanked big-time. I can't understand it. One minute, it was up by two, the next, down by ten. My guess is that it's a soured subprime loan issue, but it could just be a poor review of stock option grants. It's frustrating, you know. That feeling that there's nothing you can do to resolve a situation."

Rose flashed a wishy-washy grin. Dance was—had always been—her life. Aside from his sense of helplessness with which she was intimately acquainted, he might as well have been speaking Chinese.

"You didn't understand a bit of what I just said, did you?"

"Nope," she said with a surprisingly easy grin. "I didn't get a single word."

"That's okay. No one understands what I do. Half the time, even *I'm* confused. Hey—" he pointed to the blackened saucepan still on the stove "—I know we're supposed to be working on my dance moves, but how about grabbing a quick bite to eat first?"

Warning bells rang.

Yes, she should be professionally courteous with the man. But sharing a meal sounded suspiciously like a date.

It wasn't, though, not really.

Besides, which sounded more ominous to her already thudding heart? Being held tightly in the man's arms as he swept her across a dance floor, or sitting across a booth from him at downtown Hot Pepper's usually crowded sandwich shop?

Seeing the situation in that light put a whole new slant on the matter. By all means, she should put off dancing for as long as possible.

"Let's eat," she said, already scrambling from her chair to find her purse.

"You seem hurried. Hungry?"

"Starving."

"Great. Let's go." Holding out his hand, he hinted for her to lead the way out the loft's still-open door.

"Wait," she said, glancing at her dress. "I should change. Shoes would be a great idea, too."

"You look fine as is, but shoes are a good call."

"You think?" She couldn't help but grin on her way toward the open space designated as her bedroom. Digging through her dresser for a pair of shorts and a T-shirt, she could've sworn she'd felt the heat of his stare. She glanced his way, only to find him engrossed in one of her glossy coffee-table books on Argentina.

Good.

Again, it was understandable that she'd feel urges. John had always told her if anything ever happened to him he didn't want her spending the rest of her life alone. But it somehow felt too soon to even think of being with another man.

Clutching her clothing, she made a beeline for the bathroom—the only real room in the space aside from Anna's.

Shushing the battle raging in her head, she slipped off her dance dress, puddling the black chiffon on the tile floor. It took but a second to pull on perfectly respectable jean cutoffs that felt too short and tight and a pink, scoop-necked T-shirt that wasn't much better. Why was she feeling overexposed? She'd worn this very outfit tons of times to the grocery store and to pick up Anna from soccer practice or games.

She was being silly.

Spying her favorite leather sandals beside the hamper, she slipped her feet in, wriggled her red-tipped toes, then gave herself a quick pep talk on surviving the night.

Back in the living area, she found Mr. Montgomery still immersed in her book. When she said, "Let's go," he didn't even look at her on his way to the door. Not that she'd wanted him to!

"More comfortable?" he asked on the shadowy landing.

"Yes." See? She hadn't a thing to worry about.

Especially since her awareness of him seemed mainly one-sided. A good thing, seeing how now that she knew he couldn't care less about her, she could get on with the business of ignoring him.

Chapter Two

Hot damn, what a woman.

Outside, Dalton tried being nonchalant about sucking in the blessedly cool air. Never had there been a better time for Mother Nature to turn down the temperature. Rose had looked beautiful in her dancing dress, but the outfit she'd changed into gave him the craziest urge to grab her hand and run wild through the streets.

As hard as he'd tried focusing on that coffee-table book he'd picked up back in her apartment, his mind was stuck on one undeniable fact. Rose Vasquez was on fire. Her every move oozed slow, fiery heat that balled in his stomach, threatening to cut off his breath if he didn't put some major space between them.

"Big Daddy's Deli, okay?" he asked. "I could really go for a turkey on rye."

"Perfect," she said, shifting her thick black ponytail from the nape of her neck, exposing tantalizing, sweat-moistened curves. "Only I'm thinking I'll probably have a pastrami and Swiss."

"Yeah. Um, sure. Sounds delicious. Lead the way."

After a flashed smile, she took off.

Too bad for him, facing her backside hardly worsened the view. The sight of her perfectly rounded derriere encased in denim short shorts almost did him in. Worse yet, as if her cutoffs weren't sexy enough, her top was scant, too. Scant enough that her every step caused it to ride up, exposing a strip of tanned, firm back that he could only imagine—

No. This had to stop. He was with this woman for one reason. To learn a simple dance. Simple, simple, simple.

After Carly, he no longer associated with artsy women.

"Oh," she said, lyrically spinning, walking backward as she talked. "I've got to have raspberry tea, too. Big Daddy's makes the best in town. Perfect on a hot day or night."

Hot? Did someone say hot? Picturing his instructor running a frosted glass across her glowing collarbone scorched him. And no way was tea going to be enough to cool him down.

"You okay?" she asked. "You look—" she cocked her head, causing that ponytail of hers to tumble in a glorious wave across her left shoulder "—kind of flushed."

"I'm fine," he said, quickening the pace. "Just a little out of shape." Right. He worked out five days a week. He'd never been in better shape. Problem was, he'd also never been in better-shaped company.

Business. Think business.

No other topic held the power to so quickly bring him down.

"Mr. Montgomery?" Rose abruptly stopped. Pirouetted to face him.

As deep in thought as he was, Dalton crashed into her. Only this wasn't the kind of collision one called the police about. More like paramedics. Sounded corny, but from the moment his body bumped into hers, he needed CPR.

Her breasts… Sweet warmth mounded against his chest. Her smell… Musky, mysterious, exotic. Damp tropical earth after an afternoon rain. Had there ever been a woman more worthy of poetic verses?

The fact that he'd even thought such a thing had him breathing unsteadily. He wasn't supposed to like poetry. How many times during his formative years had his father told him poetry—any art, for that matter—was for wimps not future executives?

"Sorry," he said, lurching back.

"That's okay. It was my fault for stopping. You just had this determined stride, like you were going to keep walking."

"Right. So, see? The crash was my fault for not keeping my eyes on the road." *Instead of your behind.*

"Hey," she said, holding open the restaurant's door, "don't sweat it. Once we get started on our lessons, we'll get a lot closer than that."

Dalton gulped.

Thank the good Lord for the air-conditioned breeze

streaming from the restaurant. The rich smell of mingled cold cuts and cheeses further revived him.

His companion asked, "How's that table?"

He glanced in the direction she'd pointed.

An intimate table for two. The windowed alcove would've been ideal if this were a date, but since it wasn't, and he didn't want to risk another medical emergency, he stammered, "I'm, a...touch claustrophobic. How about that one?" He gestured toward a well-lit booth large enough to seat eight and sandwiched between a rowdy family of five and the beeping cash register.

After they sat across from each other, a waitress stopped by and they both ordered raspberry tea.

Once the pretty teen had returned with their drinks, then left them to study menus, Ms. Vasquez said, "I never can decide whether to get the pastrami and Swiss or try something new. It's a toss-up, you know. One way's safe, comfortable. The other's a risk. Calculated, but a risk all the same."

Dalton took a hasty sip of tea. Could the woman read minds? Only he hadn't been pondering his food selection, but his life choices. What was it about the woman that'd made him itchy? Discontent?

"I'll have the pastrami," she said. "I just can't help it. It's so good." She slid her menu to the end of the table. "How about you? Made a decision?"

"My usual turkey on rye." *I'm not in the mood for experimentation.* Though the night had started out on the fun side—kind of a wild departure from his usual

staid evenings of *Seinfeld* reruns and frozen dinners—
Rose's offhand comment about risk taking had re-
minded him that after being badly burned nearly a
decade ago, he'd taken few chances in his own life.

So what? Did that make him less a man for choosing
the path of least resistance? Because from where he
was sitting, that's how he suddenly felt. He sighed.

After ordering, Rose asked, "Everything all right?"

"Sure," he said. Peachy. At least it would be once this
dance thing was over.

"You seem tense. Did I say something to offend you?"

"No. Just a rough day at work dogging me."

"Want to talk about it? I mean, not to be nosy, but our
dancing will go easier if we're at least friends."

Considering how a few minutes earlier he'd wanted to
take their acquaintance beyond friendship, Dalton had a
tough time meeting her gaze. The woman was only trying
to be professionally courteous, yet from the moment
they'd met, his thoughts had been anything but professional. "You know how I mentioned I work at the bank?"

"Mmm… Fun." The sparkle in her eyes told him she
was teasing.

He flashed her a wry grin. "It can be. When the
money's flowing…"

"Why do I get the impression there's a but on the end
of that statement?" She still smiled, but her eyes now
looked sad. "Mr. Montgomery, as much as you may
like to have folks believe otherwise, I don't think you're
all about the Benjamins."

Her statement hit him hard. How could she know something like that? Something he'd never admitted to anyone, yet a fact that'd troubled him for years. What kind of banker could he be when he didn't live and breathe money?

"Sorry," she said after the waitress left homemade chips and fat dill pickles. "My friend Rachel and I are always playing games like that. You know, trying to figure out deep, dark secrets about people just by looking at them. I didn't mean anything by it."

Dalton knew he should be relieved by her statement, but how could he be when this stranger's guess had been right on the mark? Taking a chip, he asked, "What about me—my appearance—led you to this conclusion?"

"Really wanna know?"

To deflect the fact that he didn't just *want* to know, but *had* to, he chuckled. "Just curious."

Reaching across the table for his wrist, she tapped his clear plastic watch face. "*This* is a dead giveaway."

"What?"

"Your Fossil." On a business trip to New York City, he'd picked it up at the gift shop in the Met. For college graduation, he'd been presented with a gold-and-diamond Rolex, but something about the sand and mini fossils inside this cheap black model made him smile. "Just my opinion, here, but no man obsessed with money would be caught dead wearing such a fun yet unpretentious timepiece."

He snatched a pickle, bit off a big chunk and chewed.

"Ah…" She eased back against the red vinyl booth and grinned. "I'll take that as a sign I'm right."

"You can take it as a sign to mind your own business."

"Sorry," she said, and her earnest expression told him she meant it. "For the record, I like your watch. And I'm sure you're a fine banker—regardless of your lack of gold or a silk tie."

The waitress brought their sandwiches.

"Well?" Rose urged, pastrami held to her mouth. "Say something."

"I'm not sure what to say. You apparently know everything." He dug into his sandwich, glad he'd gone with the safe old standby.

"Oh, now, don't be like that. I said sorry. It's just a game. I didn't mean anything by it."

"Did I say you did?"

"You're sure acting like I did. Like I touched a nerve. If so, really, I'm sorry."

"Forget it. Just eat, so we can get on with our lesson."

"Wait…" Her big brown eyes widened. "Was I right? Do you secretly hate your job and feel guilty about it?"

"Is it any of your business if you were right?"

"No, but…" She nibbled her sandwich. "Again, sorry. But if I *was* right, then you couldn't be in a better place. Not the deli, but starting dance class. Dancing is a wonderful way to release tension, and beyond that, to discover yourself. You know, really and truly—"

"Look, I hate to rain on your dance parade, but can we just eat and get on with it?"

"NO, MR. MONTGOMERY, I said walk, not romp." Rose rolled her eyes and sighed. Had she really only a few hours earlier guiltily looked forward to dancing with this man? The same man who'd been a grump at dinner and had already broken half her toes and was now working on the other five?

With dramatic flair, he raised his hands in the air, then smacked them against his thighs. "I don't know what you want from me. First, you're telling me to walk, then pivot. Go in a straight line, then a box. Honestly, woman, the only place I feel like going is straight out the door!"

"Fine! Just do that!"

"Okay, I will!"

By this time, they stood toe-to-toe, chest-to-chest, and while Rose's fingertips itched to shake the attitude out of him, at the same time, their heated arguing had raised her blood pressure to an all-out boil that felt closer to passion than fury.

Exertion had them both breathing hard, and as their gazes locked, the sight of this powerfully built man getting worked up over an easy *giro* turn sequence was all she needed to spark a giggle.

"What's so funny?" he asked.

"You. *Us.*" She flopped her hands at her sides, then glanced at the studio wall clock. "It's past nine. No wonder we're both on edge." Most evenings, she'd long since tucked Anna into bed and was well on her way herself. At least until her racing mind stole any chance for a decent night's rest.

Eyes closed, he arched his head back and sighed. "You're right. Sorry."

"Me, too." And she was. Mostly about the fact that if she were truthful, a big part of Dalton Montgomery's dancing troubles weren't caused by him, but her. She needed to loosen up. "We seem to spend an awful lot of time apologizing."

"I've noticed." He dry-washed his face with his hands.

"We don't have to learn everything in one night. What's your hurry?"

"Heard of Miss Hot Pepper?"

"Sure," she said with a nod on her way to a compact fridge. Grabbing a bottled water, she asked, "That's the queen crowned at the pageant held in conjunction with the Hot Pepper Festival, right?"

He eyed her drink. "Got another one of those?"

She handed him a bottle. "Well?"

"What?"

"Your hurry?"

"I have to dance at the pageant. During that awkward downtime while the judges tally their scores. It's really stupid, and—"

"Why do you say that?"

"What?"

"That it's stupid? The tango. There you go again, insulting a beautiful art form out of ignorance, or—"

"I'm not insulting it. I just don't want to know it. I

resent like hell being told I have to waste Lord only knows how many nights in this studio when I could be home—"

"What?" she challenged, hands on her hips. "What sounds more fun than dancing?"

"Digging ditches."

Rolling her eyes, she said, "You haven't even given tango a chance." *Why do I even care?* The smart choice would be to let him walk. But if he chose to make a buffoon of himself in front of the entire town, so be it. "For that matter, there are things I'd rather be doing than standing around here arguing with a guy who'd rather be waist deep in muck."

"Who are we kidding?" He set his water against the baseboard, then massaged his temples. "I don't have a dancing bone in my body. Not even a dancing cell. Do you really think it's even possible for me to learn to tango?"

His admission of vulnerability not only surprised her, but warmed her. She knew all too well what it was like to feel incapable of learning something. Only in her case, it'd been basic life skills. After John's death, she'd handled things like paying bills and scheduling car maintenance. Being able to sleep alone in her and John's king-size bed—that she hadn't yet tackled.

"I not only think it's possible for you to tango," she said, warring with her stinging eyes to keep tears at bay, "I know."

Sashaying to the stereo, she selected a favorite Latin CD, then cranked the volume. When the walls pulsed with the music's life, she held out her arms. "It is customary for the man to ask the woman to dance, but since you seem to be feeling a bit shy, how about it? Care to escort me on a trip around the dance floor?"

She didn't give him a chance to answer.

In the time span of two beats, she placed one hand on his bicep and held her other up, palm out for him to meet. Her palm kissing his, Rose willed her pulse to slow. Eyes closed, lips slightly parted, she listened for the beat. Remembered what it used to be like onstage with John in the moment before the curtain rose…

Earlier, admitting she found her new student attractive had been easy. Being held in his unexpectedly capable arms while the beat she and her husband had so loved pulsed all around them was proving impossible.

Stopping, hands to her forehead, Rose said, "That's enough for tonight."

"But—"

She marched to the stereo, turning it off. The resulting silence was deafening.

"Everything okay?"

"Of course." Turning her back to him, Rose swiped a few sentimental tears. Though she'd danced the tango with other men since John's death, something about this man's provocative hold made the dance different. Special.

"Then why are you crying?"

He'd crept up behind her. He stood close enough that his radiated heat scorched her, but he didn't touch her. For that she was vastly relieved. It'd been so long since she'd shared another human's—a man's—touch. Oh sure, she hugged Rachel and Anna all the time, but somehow it wasn't the same. In her new student, she sensed a hidden gentle quality she suspected he preferred to hide. But that was dance's magic. It stripped a man—or woman—to the soul, baring innermost secrets for even a casual partner to see. Dalton's touch had been tentative. Soft. Respectful. All of which was good, but at the same time bad. For those qualities were the very things urging her to spin around for a hug.

"Rose?" It was the first time he'd called her by her first name. He made the word lovely. Delicate. "I know my dancing's bad. But surely not bad enough to reduce you to tears."

His stab at humor made her smile, then cry all the harder. She ran to the hall for privacy, but to her horror, Dalton followed.

Hand on her left shoulder, he asked, "What's wrong?"

"Nothing," she said, needing to be away from this man, from the overwhelming physical confusion being near him evoked. "I'm sorry, but our lesson is over."

"But—"

"I'm sorry," she said again, more for her own benefit than his. "I just can't."

"Do you still want me to come tomorrow night?"

She shook her head, then nodded before dashing off to the stairs leading to her loft.

Chapter Three

"Tell me, son," Dalton's father asked over the phone the next morning. "How did your dance lesson go? Are you going to make the family proud?"

"My lesson?" Let's see, considering the fact that his dancing had been so bad his teacher had run from the studio in tears, it couldn't have gone better. Dalton held the phone in one hand, and a family-size jug of antacid in the other. "It was swell. I'm thinking one more session ought to be all I need to get the hang of it."

"You're joking, right? You can't possibly expect me to believe you learned the tango in one night. The first year I performed at the pageant, it took me a good six weeks to get the hang of all those twists and turns."

Could a guy OD on antacid? Dalton scanned the label before taking another swig. "I get the one, two, three walk thing. What else is there?"

"Everything. You have to *feel* the music. Absorb it into your body and soul. According to Miss Gertrude, you have to let the music take your heart where it wants you to go."

It took everything in Dalton not to choke. "Have you been taking your medication? How is it that the man who once told me to shut off my heart is now telling me to listen to it?"

"Yes, well…" His old man cleared his throat. "That was before all this mess that's landed me on my keister. I'm currently of the opinion that it's all right to feel a little something—at least if the touchy-feely stuff lands you that much closer to achieving your business goals."

Dalton rolled his eyes.

A certain raven-haired instructor had put it a bit more meaningfully than that, and look where that speech had left him. Not merely listening to his heart, but looking deep into Rose's sultry brown eyes, then watching her burst into tears. Logic told him there had to be more to the waterworks than him, but what?

"Dalton? You still there, son?"

Unfortunately. "Yeah, Dad. I'm here."

"Good. Listen up. Not to put any added pressure on you, but my ticker's not getting better, and watching the festival I founded go off without a hitch means a lot. Your mother and I both are looking forward to your performance. Miranda, too. Do I make myself clear?"

"Crystal."

After pressing the phone's off button, Dalton reached for a pencil, then snapped it in half.

Do I make myself clear?

God, he was so sick of hearing that phrase.

Especially in regard to the not-so-subtle hints that he settle down with Miranda Browning—a woman he'd known since they'd both been kids. Their parents thrust them together at every possible moment, and while Dalton enjoyed her company as a friend, that was it. More than a few times, his mom had suggested Dalton marry Miranda.

At first, the notion had been ludicrous, but lately, he'd begun wondering if maybe his parents were right. Especially considering what a disastrous choice he'd made when following his own heart.

FRIDAY NIGHT, Dalton arrived at the dance studio, stomach churning. He wasn't sure what to expect. Would his teacher be the teary-eyed wreck he'd last seen, or the fireball with whom he'd shared dinner?

He entered Hot Pepper Dance Academy not sure he even wanted to be there. He had enough of his own troubles. Did he really want the added burden of someone else's?

The lobby was deserted.

From the studios came the muted beats of tangos and sambas. Or were those mambos and salsas? Before he had the chance to decide, a rowdy bunch of women stampeded through the glass door of studio three. Sweaty women. Women with messy nests for hair and lifeless sweatsuits for costumes. They looked fresh from gym class.

Rose emerged looking as if she'd spent a night

dancing between the sheets. Her skin wasn't blotchy from exertion, but glowing. Her hair didn't look tangled, but tousled. Her formfitting, fire-orange dress was every male's fantasy. As for her endless legs? He forced a deep breath. *Don't even get started.*

"Mr. Montgomery," she said, her voice raspy. "I'm so glad you decided to give tango another try."

To hell with the tango. I'm here to see you. To solve the mystery behind your tears.

"Sure. I'm, ah, looking forward to getting back on the proverbial horse."

"Wonderful." Red-tipped fingers singeing his forearm, she graced him with her smile. So, she'd reverted to fireball status. "Let me reschedule these ladies for next week, then I'll be right with you."

Her touch had been casual. After she flitted from him, she used the same friendly gesture on five different people, but somehow, that didn't matter. Nothing mattered but that his arm still hummed with her heat.

Forcing a deep breath, reminding himself he wasn't here for a date, but to fulfill a business obligation, Dalton aimed for the studio the women had just left. He groaned when the space still smelled of Rose's tropical perfume. The rich scent brought to mind orchids. Ocean. Hot sand. Even hotter bodies glistening with coconut-scented oil.

He swallowed hard.

"There you are." The teacher, in all her raven-haired, full-lipped glory strolled through the door. "I'd hoped you hadn't escaped."

"Not for lack of wanting," he managed to say with a wry smile.

"Tsk, tsk. What kind of attitude is that for our second lesson?"

Why did you run from our first lesson crying? he longed to ask. Instead, he shrugged.

"Well?" She clapped her hands, rubbing them together as if she was looking forward to the coming hour. "Should we jump right in, or would you like to spend a few minutes reviewing what you've already learned?"

"Let's dive," he said, trying not to feel hurt about her apparently having no wish to tell him what had been wrong the previous night.

"Excellent." Thrilled to be done with the small talk that had her heart racing, Rose escaped to the stereo. She was careful to play a more lively tune than the one that'd reduced her to tears. True, all tangos followed the same basic beat, but the moods changed.

When "La ultima cita" began, she said, "All right, Mr. Montgomery, now I'm going to really challenge you."

He sighed.

"This isn't the time to cop an attitude. All I'm asking you to do is dance backward."

"What?"

"You heard me." She stopped in front of him, adopting the classic pose with her hand on his upper arm. "Imagine we're in a vast ballroom filled with dancers. There will be young men impressing the girls with their fancy footwork, still-in-love grandparents following rhythms it's taken them a lifetime to absorb. And then, there's us…" She took a deep breath, offered what she hoped was an encouraging grin. "Feel like giving it a try?"

He grudgingly gave in and half an hour and a lot of laughter later, Rose and Dalton were moving about the floor like pros. Well, not quite, but at least they hadn't tripped over each other in the past few minutes.

Rose closed her eyes and let the music and feel of his arms transport her not to her familiar grief, but to a smoky club in the heart of old-town Buenos Aires. What fun she would have showing this uptight banker how to loosen up.

Their chemistry was intoxicating. But as badly as she longed to be held in a man's arms, she was afraid of opening her heart again only to potentially lose it.

Despite the warning, the part of her that longed to laugh and play and dance, not because it was her job, but for the sheer joy of it, urged her to spend more time with Dalton.

When they were both out of breath, Rose pulled away with a gleeful clap. "That was so much better!"

"It was?"

"Absolutely." Even as she laughed and playfully swatted him, Rose wished her breathing would return to normal. Though Dalton had still made plenty of mistakes, something about his style was intrinsically rhythmic. Like her, though he might not know it, he'd been born with an artist's soul. Once he'd lost his fierce scowl of determination and allowed his mind and heart to go where the music took him, he'd easily fallen into the spirit of the dance. "Ready to go again?"

"I think so."

"You think?" She shook her head. "No, no. You should say, of course," she said with a grin.

For the first time in she couldn't remember when, she was having fun and didn't want the night to end.

She ignored her earlier misgivings, choosing to enjoy herself. Soon enough, she'd be back upstairs with Anna, fighting to sleep through the night. Maybe if she exerted herself rest would come more easily.

That in mind, she inserted a new CD, putting herself and her student through rigorous moves.

"Whew." Twenty minutes later, again out of breath, Rose pulled away, reaching for a towel she'd hung from the ballet bar. "I'd say you've gone as far as you can with *la caminita.*"

"And that would be?"

"All that means, is *the walk,* which is the most basic of all tango steps. Now that you're walking, we can start to run."

"Great," he said with a chuckle. "And I suppose we're going to start that running right now, Miss Energizer Bunny?"

"Ha-ha." With her towel, she swatted him. "Actually, you and I are done for today. I have a date."

"A date, huh? Is he the cause of last night's tears?"

For a second after Dalton asked the question, Rose felt like a deer in the headlights. What was she supposed to say? Was now the time to tell him about her husband?

"Hey," he murmured, tone soft, as if he sensed her distress. "Why you were crying is really none of my business." He glanced down, then looked back up into her eyes. "Trouble is, I kind of took the whole *our dancing will go easier if we're friends* speech seriously, and seeing how friends don't let friends cry alone, I—"

"My date is with my daughter. She wants to bake sugar cookies with pink sprinkles."

"You have a little girl? I mean, I assume she's *little,* judging by your age."

"My *advanced* age?" With a wink and grin, she swatted him with her towel again.

For a moment he stilled, as if he wanted to say something, but propriety kept him quiet. "That's not at all what I meant, and you know it."

"Yes, I do," she said with a nod, matching his easy smile. "And in answer to your question…"

"I didn't ask a question."

"Your eyes did." She turned her back on him while wrapping herself in a hug. The kindness in Dalton's eyes told her it was safe to share her pain with him. "My girl is indeed little. She's six. And in answer to your unspoken question, her father…died."

"Sorry," he said quietly. She imagined him cupping his warm, strong hands over her shoulders, infusing her with much needed courage to go on. Instead, he hovered, not taking the liberty of actually touching her, but letting her know he was there. "Is he the reason for those tears?"

She nodded. "The last time I seriously tangoed— you know, beyond teaching vacation-bound senior citizens or Girl Scout troops—was in his arms. So you can see where…"

"Dancing again—with a man—would be rough?" He did touch her shoulder then, and lightly turned her to face him. The warmth of his eyes and tender set of his mouth, his solid yet gentle grip, told her what words never could. That he cared. That she wasn't alone. Sure, she had friends, but no one with whom she'd ever considered sharing the depth of her pain.

"Want to talk about him?" he invited.

"Yes. Someday. But not now."

"Sure."

"It's not that I don't want to tell you about him, just that it hurts to dredge up the past."

"I get it. Only, the way you were crying, I'm thinking your husband's death isn't yet in the past—at least not where your heart's concerned."

"ANNA, HONEY, be careful or you'll drop Barbie's purse behind the display."

"I'm being careful, Mommy. Look! She's dancing!"

Dalton froze at the entry to Bell's. He had been dreading the mission to get fitted for the gaudy red shoes he was required to wear with his equally hideous tux. But from his first sight of Rose and her cute, brown-eyed daughter, trying on black-patent Mary Janes, his outlook on the mission had miraculously brightened.

"Ladies' day out?" he asked the pair, pausing in front of the battered, red-carpeted platform serving as seating for what Mona Bell had dubbed her kid zone.

"Hi," Rose said, her wide grin making his pulse race. "My baby's feet seem to get bigger every day."

"I know the feeling," he teased, wagging one of his size thirteens.

Her daughter giggled. "You've got the biggest feet I've ever seen."

"Anna!" the girl's mother scolded.

"It's okay," Dalton said with a chuckle. "Especially since it happens to be true."

"There *are* bigger feet in this town," Mona said, a hint of her Cajun heritage flavoring her words. In her arms were three shoe boxes. "Dalton, nice to see you finally showed up. If we don't get your shoe order in pronto, you'll be dancing barefoot."

"Sounds like an improvement over the getup you all want me to wear."

Snorting, Mona said, "Remind me to tell your momma what a misfit she raised."

"She hears it all the time."

Ignoring him, Mona turned to Rose's daughter. "Stick out your feet, there, toots, and let me slip these on."

"She's a cutie," Dalton said to Rose, seeing how Mona had pretty much taken over the operation.

"Thanks."

"Anna's a nice name. I've always liked it."

"We named her after my grandmother, Anna Lucia Margarita Rodriguez. In her day, she was the darling of Buenos Aires." Whispering behind her hand, she added, "She reportedly juggled up to ten suitors with ease."

Mona grunted. "Shoot, what gal in her right mind would want that many men?"

"Barbie!" Anna squealed, pirouetting the doll in a dazzling move that sent tiny pink plastic shoes and a matching purse flying. They landed behind the seating platform. "Oops."

"Oh, honey," Rose said, hands on her hips. "I told you that was going to happen."

Tears flooded the child's eyes. "I'm sorry, Mommy."

"It's okay." Already on his knees, Dalton finagled himself into torturous contortion that with gritted teeth and a grunt netted one shoe. Then he used a nearby display rack's metal prong to fish out the spiked pink heel's mate and the purse. "Voila," he said, winded from the ordeal.

"You got 'em!" Anna squealed happily, leaping from the platform to wrap her arms around him. The simple gesture warmed him to the core. He'd always loved kids, had planned on having a half dozen of his own by now, but time had a way of vanishing.

"Thank you," Anna said, her brown eyes serious.

"You're welcome," he said, giving her a brief return hug.

Mona butted into his shining moment with, "You've got fuzz balls on top of your head."

"They're cute." Rose tenderly picked them free, holding them in the palm that only last night she'd pressed against his. "Thanks again. You don't know trauma till you've lost your favorite Barbie purse."

"In that case, I'm glad tragedy could be averted."

"How about these?" Mona asked, gesturing to Anna's latest pair of shoes. "They seem like the best fit."

"What do you think, sweetie? Can you walk around?"

Instead of walking, the girl ran, skipped and pranced.

"Wish I had half that energy…" Grinning, Mona crossed her arms.

"Amen," Dalton and Rose said in unison, then laughed.

"Want those?" Mona asked.

"Yes, please."

"Good choice. Cash, check or plastic?"

While Rose paid and Anna continued to dance around the store in her new shoes, Dalton tried, unsuccessfully, to focus on his own footwear crisis. Rose consumed him. Her laugh. Her smile. The way, when she'd stood close, fingering his hair, she'd smelled of an intriguing blend of crayons and faint, musky perfume.

"Want to join us?" she asked, suddenly by his side. "Anna's on a temporary school reprieve for the dentist, but I thought since we were right here, I'd also grab her shoes before getting her back."

"Join you for what?" he asked, mesmerized by the way her hair reflected the midday sun streaming through the windows.

What the hell was wrong with him? Here he was

supposed to be heading back to work, yet all he really wanted to do was finger those inky strands. Could they be anywhere near as soft as they looked?

"There you go again," she teased, "looking as if you'd rather be anywhere but here."

"No," he said. "You've got me all wrong. I've always *adored* shoe shopping."

"Liar," she said with a soft elbow to his ribs. "Join us for a quick sandwich at the deli?"

Yes. "Sounds great, but I'm due back at the office. The only reason I'm here is that according to my fellow pageant-committee members, my shoe fitting had to be done ASAP."

"I get that, but can't your office spare you for lunch?"

"Ordinarily they could, but seeing how it's a lunch meeting I'm supposed to be at, they might frown on me switching to your team."

"We'll be more fun," she said, hugging her daughter close.

"I don't doubt that. Rain check?"

"Absolutely."

"Come on, Mommy," Anna said, tugging Rose's hand. "Me and Barbie are hungry."

"Sounds like you'd better get going," Dalton said with a faint smile.

"She's not the only one," Mona said, butting in to his last few moments of fun. "Now, quit flirting and get on over here to try on some shoes."

Dalton groaned.

Rose grinned.

"In closing," Dalton said a week later in the bank's suffocating, windowless boardroom, "it's my recommendation that the bank dispose of all TWG assets in favor of taking a temporary shelter in bonds until such time as the market's volatility subsides. Questions?"

"Excellent report," Alice Craigmoore, the bank's VP in charge of finance, said before clearing her throat.

"I concur." The bank's chief loan officer, Bud Weathers, eased back in his chair. "Now, seeing how that was the last item on the agenda, who's up for Chinese?"

"Sounds good," Dalton said, straightening his files.

His father sighed. "I've been ordered to steer clear of the fried stuff, but I suppose they have something on the menu that's steamed."

Alice again cleared her throat. "I, um, do have one more question."

"Shoot," Dalton said.

"Mona tells me you're sweet on your tango teacher. Care to substantiate?"

Dalton closed his eyes and counted to ten.

"Son," his father interjected, "your mother told me you were seeing the Browning girl."

He cocked one eye open. "Occasionally," Dalton admitted, "but it's nowhere near as serious as Mom would like."

"There's no law that says a guy can't be hot for his teacher. Especially if she's your *hot* dance teacher," Bud confided, and winked. Dalton fought the urge to smack the suggestive look right off his face. He couldn't say why, but he felt protective toward Rose. She'd been through a seriously rough patch. Sure, she was sexy, but she was also fragile. She deserved to be treated with infinite care.

"Thank you all for your comments," Dalton said, tone brusque, "but could we please get on with lunch?"

"What's your hurry?" Bud asked with a snort. "Got an after-lunch dance lesson?"

Chapter Four

"No, no, no, Dalton!" Rose cried above the pulsing Latin beat. "I said to arch toward the door, not away from it."

"What the hell do you think I am? Made of rubber?" The minute Dalton had said the words, he regretted them. He'd never been prone to shoot his mouth off in the heat of anger, but then, this was the first time he'd felt an emotion other than boredom or resignation since his last lesson.

Rose marched to the stereo to turn off the music. Then she returned, heels punching the wood floor in the sudden silence, to stop six inches in front of him, hands on her hips. "First of all, the rock step is the mere tip of the iceberg in terms of technicalities. Second…" Frosty expression thawing, she grinned. "How can I stay mad at you when you give me that look?"

"What look?"

"That one, right there," she said, pointing to his grinning mouth. "The one where you look like an incorrigible child."

"Yeah, but a good-looking one, right?" His grin broadened into a full-blown smile.

She rolled her eyes.

"What?"

"What am I going to do with you? You're a dancing disaster."

"At our last lesson, you told me I'd improved."

"Yes, well—" turning her back to him, she aimed for the door "—I take it back. You are quite possibly the worst dancer I have ever encountered."

"Then where are you going? Obviously, I need more instruction."

"I'm going upstairs to make a salad to go along with the enchilada casserole already in the oven."

"What about me? I mean, I paid for an hour lesson."

"I'll give you a refund."

"I've got a better idea."

"Oh?" With Dalton in the hall, she flicked off the studio's lights.

"How about inviting me for dinner?"

"What?"

"You know—food, drink, conversation. Well, we don't have to converse, but I am awfully hungry, which might explain my lack of concentration."

"I don't know…" She glanced toward the loft stairs.

"Rose. It's food. What's not to know? It's not like I'm asking you on a date." *Although that's exactly what I'd like to be doing.*

"I know, but what's Anna going to think?"

"Hmm… That you invited a friend for dinner?" He shot her another grin.

"There you go again, giving me that goofy look. How am I supposed to say no?"

"You're not. At least, that's the plan."

"Oh, all right," she said. "But behave. And Anna and I will expect help with the dishes."

"You shall have it," he teased her with a formal bow.

She returned the favor with a not-so-formal swat.

FIFTEEN MINUTES LATER, Dalton found himself seated in a kid-size chair at a kid-size table. In front of him was a blob of Play-Doh that he was guessing used to be three different shades—red, green and blue—but was now a purplish-gray.

"Mr. Dalton?" Rose's wide-eyed daughter asked, hogging all the still-pure-yellow clay.

"Yes?"

"What're you making? 'Cause there's kids at my school who do way better than you—even Tommy Butler, and he eats his boogers."

"Hey, Rose," Dalton called across the loft to the kitchen where she hummed while making salad. Although he'd offered to help, she'd refused on the grounds that not only did she not want him messing up her kitchen, but it might be helpful to his dancing if he connected with his inner child. Right. The kid in him said he needed better Play-Doh colors. "Are you hearing this abuse?"

"What I'm hearing is a lot of whining. Come on, Dalton, play nice, or I'll have to sit you in time-out."

Anna whispered, "She means it, Mr. Dalton. You'd better be good, or you'll miss Mommy's cheesy supper. It's the best."

"Okay," he said, "I'll play nice, but you'll have to show me what to make."

"A horse," she said. "I like My Little Pony. Tommy Butler says they're too girlie, but I think he's gross. And anyway, he eats his—"

"I know—" Dalton said, molding his lump of clay "—boogers."

"How'd you know?"

With his right index finger, he tapped his temple. "Superhuman mind-reading skills."

"Really?"

"No, not really," Rose said, perching on her own pint-size seat to ruffle her daughter's hair. "You already told him, sweetie."

"Hey," Dalton complained. "That's cheating. Telling all my secrets like that."

"What secret?" Rose teased. "If you're going to claim to have superhuman skills, we need proof of something pretty amazing. Not just lame old mind reading."

"Yeah," Anna said. "Can you fly? Or laser beam stuff with your eyeballs? Toby Mitchell does that during math class to get out of doing addition."

"Which?" Dalton asked. "Flying or the laser thing?"

"Sometimes both," Anna said, eyes wide, expression solemn. "Ms. Marshal tells him to stop, but he won't."

"Uh-huh," Rose said with a cluck of her tongue. "Sounds like it's time for you to wash up for dinner, and quit telling fibs."

"I'm not fibbing. Honest. And anyway, Mr. Dalton never showed us his trick."

"I'm working on it," he said, messing with his clay. "How about you do what your mom asked, then I'll show you when you get back."

"Okay."

While she skipped off to the bathroom that on an earlier trip he'd noted had been retrofit to accommodate her size with primary-colored chunky stools at the sink and tub, he continued with his masterpiece.

"What're you making?" Rose asked, leaning toward him, making him crazy with her musky scent.

"Patience. You'll see."

He hadn't expected his knack for working with clay to still be there, but it was. He wasn't sure if that was good or bad. It'd been years since he'd been near the stuff, years that blurred together without distinction.

"You look like you know what you're doing."

He shrugged.

"Where would a stodgy banker like you learn to sculpt?"

"I dabbled."

She snorted. "I took a bunch of art classes in college, but, Dalton, never once did I see anyone craft a horse like that in such a short time—let alone out of ancient Play-Doh."

The only answer he had for her was a shrug. His sculpting, like what had happened with Carly, was a part of him he didn't want to get into. What was the point?

Hearing the muffled sound of the bathroom taps being turned off, he hustled, smoothing the creature's leg muscles, then using a plastic knife to work in a flowing mane, eyes and mouth.

"Wow…" Rose tentatively reached out to touch the five-inch-tall creature. "Dalton, this is exquisite."

"No biggie."

"Yes. Yes, it is. Have you worked in other mediums?"

"If you don't mind, I'd rather drop the whole subject."

"But—"

"Whoa!" Anna ran back into the room, zeroing in on his creation. "Mr. Dalton, that's cool!" She grabbed for it, but her hold was too rough, and just as quickly as Dalton had given the horse life, the little girl destroyed it. "I'm sorry," she said, lower lip trembling and tears pooling her eyes. "I didn't mean to squish him."

"It's okay," Dalton said. "No big deal. And anyway, your mom's dinner smells great. Isn't it time to eat?"

"Yeah, but can you make me another one after dinner? I wanna take it for show-and-tell. Chase Crandall would have a cow. He makes really great Play-Doh cheeseburgers and hot dogs, but you beat him way bad on animals."

"There won't be time," he said, easing up from his chair.

"Pleeeease." The girl punctuated her whine with a few hops.

"Anna," Rose said, "would you please get the salad dressings from the fridge and set them on the table?"

"But, Mommy—"

"Anna…" she warned in the universal tone all mothers use to show they mean business.

"Okay."

Once the girl trudged off, Rose quietly asked, "Mind telling me what that was all about?"

"Yes," Rose's dinner guest said in a brusque manner she'd never heard him use. "I'm sorry, Rose. But I'd really rather not talk about it."

"But I don't see what the big deal is. Seriously, Dalton, why—"

"Please," he said. "Let's just focus on enjoying the evening."

"Okay." She eased back in her chair. "Sorry I pressed."

"There's no need to be sorry. Let's just get on with eating whatever it is that smells so good."

"All done, Mommy! Can we eat?"

Rose snuck one more glance at Dalton, trying to gauge his mood, but it was too late. He'd already left the art table to meet up with Anna at the kitchen table.

Trailing behind, Rose put the incident behind her. Seven years of marriage and plenty of dates with temperamental male dancers had shown her men could be every bit as moody as women. Though she was curious about how a topic as benign as Play-Doh could upset him.

As touchy as Dalton had been earlier, dinner was filled with lighthearted banter.

After the meal, Rose helped her daughter into pajamas, then read her *Beauty and the Beast* and tucked pink floral covers up to her chin. Then she made her way back to the kitchen, finding Dalton at the sink, elbow deep in suds.

"Impressive," she said with a whistle. "You count during the day and scrub at night."

"What can I say? I'm a Renaissance man." He winked.

She melted a little more. What was it about him that drew her? Why did he feel more like a friend than a student? Why did she care that even after sharing a meal, there was sadness behind his smile?

"Want me to dry?" she asked, deciding to skirt the issue. Given time, should their friendship continue—which she hoped it would—he'd share his troubles just as she had shared hers.

He flicked bubbles at her. "Hey, thought you were going to help instead of standing around looking pretty."

"You think I'm pretty, huh?" she said with a flirty bat of her eyelashes.

"Nah." He shot her an adorable grin. "I just said that to soften you up, you know, hoping to actually get work out of you."

"Ahh… The old flattery routine. I've always been a big fan."

"Good to know," he said while she plucked a dish towel from the bottom cabinet drawer.

They worked in companionable silence, feeling more like a couple than when they were in each other's arms on the dance floor. Her husband had never been one for domestic chores. In fact, he'd insisted on always having a housekeeper to tackle what he'd labeled menial chores. She, though, found pleasure in the simple acts of preparing a meal, then washing the dishes afterward.

"Thanks for your help," she said when they'd finished.

"Sure. No problem."

"Do you do your own housework?"

"Um, yeah. Doesn't everyone except my stodgy old parents?"

"They have help?"

"A live-in maid and cook." He sighed, putting the dish soap under the sink's cabinet, as if he'd been following the same routine for years. "Always made me feel funny having someone else clean up my messes."

"I would think any sane kid would enjoy having a servant around to clean up after him."

Shrugging, he made his way to an oversize armchair. "I can see why some kids would like it, but it just didn't feel right to me."

"Sure. I understand."

"Now that you've got the scoop on my Little Lord Fauntleroy upbringing, what was your childhood like?"

Easing onto the sofa across from him, she tucked her legs under her and smiled. "My childhood was idyllic. Lots of running through sprinklers and chasing the ice-cream truck."

"You have a big family?"

"Mom, Dad, two older brothers. Grandma and Grandpa."

"All still with you?"

"Everyone save for Grandma. She passed a few years ago. Pneumonia."

"Sorry."

"Me, too. I miss her—and her sugar cookies. But Anna and I make them often. Hopefully we're keeping a little of her spirit alive."

After a few thoughtful minutes, he said, "My dad's had a couple of close calls. He has heart trouble."

"That must've been hard on you."

"Sure. But not always in the way you think."

"What does that mean?" she asked, leaning forward.

"Nothing. Sorry. I shouldn't have said anything." Taking a deep breath, he said, "Seen any good movies lately?"

"That was a thinly veiled attempt to change the subject."

"Did it work?" he asked, eyebrows raised hopefully.

"If it did, this would be the second time tonight that you've wanted to change the subject. What's up with that? Are you suddenly becoming a man of mystery?"

"Wouldn't you like to know," he said with a chuckle, pushing up from his chair.

"Where are you going?"

"Home. It's late."

"It's eight-thirty."

Faking a yawn, he said, "Hours past my bedtime."

"What are you avoiding, Dalton Montgomery?"

"Who says I'm avoiding anything? I've got a big day tomorrow."

"Okay. When do you want your next lesson?"

"I'm good."

"You don't want another?"

"That's what I said." He stood at the door, immersed in shadow. His expression was unreadable, yet the inflection in his voice was clear. Back off. But of what?

"Dalton?" She rose. "Did I do or say something that offended you?"

"No," he said, voice softened. "Of course not. I've had a great time. Your dinner was delicious—the company, too. Anna's a doll."

"Thanks."

"You're welcome. Now, I really should get going. See you around, okay?"

"Sure." Once Dalton had gone, Rose stood at the closed door, hugging herself, wondering why Dalton's leaving had caused a knot in her throat.

Chapter Five

Two days later, Rose still didn't know why she even cared that Dalton had cut their evening short. The one thing she did know was that it felt good to worry about someone other than herself for a change.

Which was why, despite a nagging voice telling her to forget Dalton Montgomery, she now found herself reaching into her red VW Jetta's backseat for the picnic basket she'd filled with tasty treats. Hopefully she could entice him out of his office, and into the sun-flooded park.

The city of Hot Pepper was small—only a population of five thousand—but its main park was on par with any she'd been to in Dallas or Houston. There were lots of big trees and grassy knolls and playground equipment for kids of all ages. A jogging trail wound its way through, and was always crowded with runners and walkers.

Rose loved spending time outdoors. She felt that it was the best way to gain clarity when she felt tense. Hopefully, Dalton would feel the same.

Inside the bank's austere, two-story black-marble-

and-forest-green lobby was where Rose's plan nose-dived. For some reason, she'd expected Dalton to be hanging out in the lobby, waiting for rescue.

And you're the woman for the job?

Seriously, what'd even given her the impression he needed to be rescued? If he did, what qualified her for the task? They hardly knew each other. After the last time they'd talked, the way he'd practically run from her, not even wanting to set up his next lesson, it was more likely he'd had quite enough of her company.

Then why was she here?

One very simple reason. Because she wanted to be.

More to the point—she wanted him.

Cheeks flaming, she put her free hand over her mouth, thanking heaven she hadn't actually said something like that out loud. Dalton was a friend. Nothing more. Okay, so he happened to be a good-looking friend. A funny, sweet, charming friend. Where was the harm in—

"May I help you?" A tall, youthful-looking man with a shock of freckles to match his red hair approached.

"Um, yes," Rose said, willing her pulse to slow. Had coming here been such a bright idea? What if Dalton truly didn't want to see her?

"Ma'am? Do you need to set up a new account?"

"Dalton," she blurted. "Is he here?"

"You mean Mr. Montgomery?" The man's eyes widened. "He's here, but he doesn't usually see customers."

"Oh—I'm not a customer, but a friend."

"Is he expecting you?"

"Not exactly, but—"

"Could you tell me who to see for ordering new checks?" A thirtysomething woman wielding a baby in a carriage, and a toddler, strolled up, thankfully occupying the inquisitive lobby guard dog.

Rose took the opportunity to slip past both, aiming for a wide staircase leading to a gallery lined with glass-walled offices. No doubt Dalton was important, and as such, would naturally have a private working space, removed from the bustling lobby.

"Ma'am!" the greeter called. "You can't just go up there without—"

Too late. She'd already reached the top of the stairs.

She then caught a lucky break in the form of brass nameplates affixed to each oak door.

Bud Weathers…

Owen Brighten…

Alice Craigmoore…

Dalton Montgomery—Vice President.

From inside came muffled shouting. "Dammit, Borden, I told you to dump it three days ago. What the hell happened?… I don't care… Look, all I'm saying is…"

Rose stood outside his partially open door, unsure of her next move.

Dalton slammed down the phone. "Simmons, I know you're lurking out there. If you've got those figures, come in. Otherwise…"

"Surprise," Rose said, swinging the wicker basket in front of her, forcing a smile.

"Rose." Dalton lurched back in his brown leather desk chair.

"You're busy. I—I shouldn't have come."

"Of course you should. It's just a shock, that's all. Seeing you is the last thing I expected." Half smiling, he stood, gestured to the basket. "What's in there?"

"Lunch. But really, if you're busy, I can come back."

"What if I want you to stay?"

Warmth crept through her like the sun. "What if what I'd really like is for both of us to go?" She shivered. "This place gives me the creeps."

Chuckling, Dalton slipped out from behind his desk. "I agree. Let's go."

"OH, NO," Dalton said an hour later, seated on a red blanket in sun-dappled shade. "I tried those chili things. I did like you said and took off my suit jacket and loosened my tie, but I draw the line at eating peppers."

"But they're good," his hostess said, the corners of her big brown eyes crinkled with mirth.

"If you happen to have a team of paramedics standing by."

"Baby," she teased.

"What I am is smart," he teased right back, intertwining his fingers with hers. She looked lovely. Full, yellow sundress tucked around her endless bronzed legs just so. Long hair wild and free, flowing in the light breeze. The park around them was vibrant spring-green, teeming with the kind of life he wasn't used to seeing on a Thursday afternoon. Chubby-fingered, laughing toddlers ran alongside swings and slides while their mothers congregated on benches drenched in sun. Birds chirped and leaves rustled and Dalton found himself aching to kiss Rose for having saved him from the office. From what had become a crushingly lonely and frustrating existence.

"Thank you," he said, giving her hands a squeeze.

"For what?" Her question rang of innocence. As if she truly didn't know how colorless his life had become.

"For the amazing lunch." He brought her hand to his mouth, turning it upside down to kiss her palm. "I'm still not sure what half the stuff was that we ate, but it was good." And it hadn't left him reaching for his antacids like he did after downing a greasy, three-meat combo from Duffy's.

"You're welcome. I'm glad you're having fun."

"Are you having fun, too?" He hadn't meant to ask, but now that the question had slipped out, he had to admit harboring a burning need to know.

"Yes," she said simply, making him feel like the luckiest man alive just to be graced by her smile. What was it about her that not only soothed but excited? Why was it that whenever he was around her, he could hardly remember to breathe? "I'm having a great time."

"You do this often?" he asked, releasing her hand,

gesturing to their surroundings. "While away whole afternoons in the park?"

"As much as I can. Lucky for me, most of my dance classes are in the late afternoon and evenings. I used to bring Anna with me to the park, but now that she's in school, my usual companion is a good book."

"Probably beats the heck out of working in an office, huh?" He winked.

Her resulting grin made him loathe his life's choices all the more. Had things gone right a decade ago, would moments like this be the norm, rather than a blazing streak of color in his otherwise gray existence?

Lying back to rest on his elbows, Dalton drank in the day. The woman. The novelty of being free of his cell phone while the sky was still blue.

"What's got you so deep in thought?" Rose asked.

"Nothing," he lied, not wanting to mar the afternoon's perfection.

"Then what's causing this?" She traced the furrow between his brows. "I've been seeing it a lot the past few minutes."

"You're not real big on letting a man keep his secrets, are you?"

"Depends," she said with a slow, sexy smile. "Are they juicy?"

He snorted. "More like boring as hell."

"Not to pry, but—"

"Yoo-hoo! Dalton! Rose!"

Groaning, he said, "Don't look now, but we've got trouble looming just over that hill."

Alice Craigmoore, decked out in a navy suit and hot-pink jogging shoes, waved again. "Hey, you two! Don't even think of pretending you don't see me." Hands on her hips, the middle-aged woman breathed hard, but not hard enough to shut her up. "Well? Dalton, does your father know you're out here picnicking instead of in your office?"

Laughing, Rose ignored his scowl, stood and extended her hand to Alice. The two women acted like long-lost friends.

Dalton used the time to reassemble himself—both in spirit and attire. Before Alice had stuck her snoopy nose into his business, he'd contemplated telling Rose everything. About the mess with Carly and the secret dreams he'd harbored before he'd met her. He would have told Rose what his father had done to ensure Dalton toed the family line, and how even now that he was older, his sense of honor prevented him following his own path. He had planned on telling her all of that, but now that he'd had a second to think about it, it was probably for the best that he kept it to himself. After all, as soon as this dancing gig was over, he'd probably only run into Rose around town.

"Dalton," Alice said, "it's good to see Rose has kept you on top of your dance lessons. I'd hate to see the entire town shamed by your lack of interest."

"He'll do an amazing job," Rose assured. "He has an inborn sense of grace that can't be taught."

"Really?" Alice's eyebrows shot up. "Our Dalton? A

natural dancer? Judging by his father's two left feet, I never would've guessed."

"I haven't had the pleasure of meeting Dalton's dad, but surely he's also been graced with the dancing gene?"

"No," Alice said with a firm shake of her head. "Make no mistake, the man *thinks* he's Fred Astaire, but his past performances have been more along the lines of *Sesame Street*'s Big Bird."

"Hey," Dalton warned, under a family obligation to ensure his father was given adequate credit for his moves, "Dad's got skills."

"Right," Alice said with a good-natured cackle. "He's quite adept at making his partners cry."

"Oh, now," Rose said, "I don't believe that for a second."

"Believe what you will," Alice said, "but I'll rest a lot easier knowing Dalton's dance instruction's in good hands. Have fun!" With a backhanded wave, the woman was thankfully on her way.

"I should've remembered she goes for a jog in the park most every afternoon," Dalton moaned.

"The few times I've met her around town, she's always seemed nice," Rose said.

"If you like chatting up bulls. I hate how she's placed herself in charge of the proverbial playground. Especially mine."

"Oh," she said, gathering up the remains of their meal, "I think she was just making conversation. I wouldn't make too big a deal of it."

"Why are you always doing that?"

"What?" She froze while putting away a stack of orange napkins.

"Looking on the bright side. Especially after the crappy hand life dealt you. Don't you ever just want to rail?"

"What point would that serve? Being angry at the world isn't going to change anything. Why not just make the best of what you've been given?"

Sounded simple enough in theory, but seeing how Dalton had been doing just that for the past decade, he'd grown tired of pretending everything was okay. Never more so than now, when a few brief meetings with Rose Vasquez had shown him just how much his life had been missing. He wanted boisterous family dinners and playing with his own sweet little girl. He wanted more picnics and laughter and afternoons at the park. He wanted all of that, but being an only child, he'd inherited a legacy it was his duty to fulfill.

Ha. That's a good line, but now, how about the truth? That for all of Rose's attributes, she was fundamentally different from him. She was an artist. He was an artist-wannabe.

"It's back," Rose said, tracing his furrow. "Are you ever going to tell me what's going on in that thick head of yours?"

"Wait, the other night, I said you have a pretty head, and now, instead of telling me I have a handsome mug, all you can say is that it's thick?"

She smoothed his hair. "It's an adorably thick head. Does that make you happy?"

Not especially. What would make him happy? Distracting Rose with a lingering kiss.

"Hmm…" Drawing her lower lip into her mouth, she said, "since you're back to scowling, I guess that compliment doesn't especially thrill you."

She was wrong about that.

THE MORNING SUN seemed to slice Dalton's office in two.

Darkness and light. It was fitting, considering his mood.

Tossing his briefcase on one of a matching set of burgundy wingback guest chairs, he then flopped into his own seat. On autopilot, he reached for the jug of antacid in his top-right desk drawer.

Bottle clutched to his chest, he leaned back as far as he could go, closing his eyes. He wished washing away confusion was as easy as taking a dose of medicine.

His whole adult life had been built around the concept that it was noble for him to put aside any personal dreams or goals for the sake of his family. He'd tried things his way and failed. Now, the smart thing to do was buckle down and accept his lot in life. Maybe even take a second look at Miranda—or a woman like her. But lately, everything he'd once thought set in stone had changed.

He'd once harbored resentment toward his father, for having boxed him into this life. But now, after spending time with Rose and Anna, Dalton wondered if maybe part of the reason he and his father had never been all that close was that his dad had been so busy putting in fourteen-hour days, that he'd never had time for anything else. Never once had his father sat down with him to play the way Dalton had the other night with Anna. For that matter, did his dad even know how to play?

Hands cupping his forehead, Dalton closed his eyes, releasing a deep sigh.

What was wrong with him?

Drudging up all this personal stuff?

Was he really saying he was unhappy with his life because *Daddy* hadn't played Hot Wheels with him? That was ridiculous.

Dalton was a grown man. If he wanted to walk away from the bank, from the cell housing him each day from seven to six, he could.

But because he was a better man than that, because he'd been taught to honor his obligations, he wouldn't leave his family in the lurch. Anyway, he'd tried making a living from his art when he was with Carly, but never seemed to have made enough of an income to provide a decent life.

Of course, now, he had plenty of savings to live comfortably for quite a while without needing to work. What if that'd been the only thing missing from his previous attempt to lead an artist's life? Time. The chance to build up enough of an inventory to put on an amazing studio show.

As for the woman who'd brought these rebellious

thoughts swelling to the forefront of his mind? She was beautiful, bright, talented and funny. Sexy as hell. Yet from the way his emotions had been in constant turmoil since meeting her, it was also pretty obvious that she was trouble.

Yeah…

Trouble he couldn't wait to be with again.

Chapter Six

"You decided to give tango another whirl?"

Dalton shrugged. Even if Rose Vasquez was bad for him, he didn't have the self-control to stay away.

She ducked her gaze, her expression hidden by her sleek fall of dark hair. "Considering our last lesson, I didn't figure you'd come."

"Me, neither. But after work, I climbed into my car, and the damn thing headed this way."

"Hmm… You might want to see a mechanic about that."

"Yeah," he said with a faint chuckle.

"You okay?" Her voice was so soft, so tender and brimming with genuine concern. He was definitely *not* okay.

"Sure. Great." The lobby fountain merrily tinkled, reminding him that this was a dance lesson he faced, not a firing squad. Just because he'd wound up here yet again didn't mean he was quitting his job or running off to *find himself.* All it meant was that he wanted to make his family and friends proud.

"I'm glad. Though you seem down. Rough day at the office?"

He shrugged, shoving his hands in his pockets to stop his fingertips from tucking her hair behind her ears. He wanted to see her face. Her beautiful eyes. "I guess it was no worse than usual."

"That much fun, huh?"

After casting her a faint grin, he shook his head.

"Okay, well…" She tipped back her head, granting him full access to her lovely face, filling him not only with crazy urges to kiss her, but sculpt her, as well. He wanted to freeze her impossible beauty in time. The very notion was stupid. One Play-Doh horse did not a sculptor make. He'd never do her justice. "Honestly, I didn't think you were coming, so I didn't even work out a plan of attack."

"That's okay," he said. "How about we just skip it? You could probably use the time with Anna."

"I had a light afternoon. We went to the park and we made fajitas for an early supper. Her sitter, Kelly's, with her now, watching a movie. So if it's all right, I'd very much like to be with you—one of my more special students."

She smiled, and the force of it took him back to when he'd been a kid, schlepping his way through college. Free to explore all of life's delicious flavors. Back then, as now, Rose would've been at the top of his most requested list of forbidden fruits.

"*Special,* huh?" She'd headed for the door of studio three, and he trailed after her, enjoying the view. Her low-cut, black leotard clung to her and showed off all her curves. "I like the sound of that much better than *dance challenged.*"

"Hey," Rose said, "don't sell yourself short. You did a great job at our last session." *Almost as good as the job I'm doing of pretending I'm not thrilled you're here.* The knowledge that Dalton stood only a few feet behind her made it difficult to breathe.

Pushing open the studio door, she welcomed the room's air-conditioned chill washing over her flushed chest and cheeks. Only when she stood in the center of the brightly lit space, when the cool air had cleared her mind and heart and she once again felt like a highly qualified dance instructor instead of a giddy teen, did she say, "Here's what I think we ought to do."

Her thoughts had been clear, but then he removed his jacket, flooding her with the rich scents of leather and him. He wore black jeans and a formfitting black T-shirt that hugged powerful biceps she knew from their last lesson were rock hard to the touch.

She licked her lips and tucked her hair behind her ears. *Think, Rose. You've taught dozens of students how to tango. Dalton's just a man. The sooner you teach him this dance, the sooner he'll be out of your life.*

But then maybe that was her biggest problem. She didn't want him out of her life, but ever deeper in it.

"Rose?" he asked. "Everything okay?"

"Of course." In fact, on the verge of stepping into his arms, her once-brittle life felt alarmingly okay. Which, judging by her thundering pulse, could be a problem. Enough. She had to focus. "Music would probably be a good place for us to start," she said, already on her way to the stereo. "Then I want to try something new. At your previous lessons, I'm afraid I put too much emphasis on learning the rules rather than absorbing the true essence of the dance. If you don't feel it, it will be impossible for you to learn the embellishments that will make your version of the tango truly stand out among the rest. Make no mistake, you've come a long way since our first session, but I want to be certain you've internalized the beat." Slipping one of her favorite CDs, *Yo soy el Tango,* into the stereo, she pressed Play. "Does that make sense?"

"Of course." *Liar.* Dalton dragged in air. Right about now, the only thing that would make sense was to not walk but run from this situation as fast as his legs would carry him. "You're making perfect sense."

"Wonderful. Let's start off by having you take the lead, walking backward to the music." She stepped toward him. "Remember, you place your fingers here…" Encircling his wrist, she slipped his hand behind her, settling it on the small of her back. "Then I'm going to put my hand here… On your upper arm. Remember this position?"

Lord, yes. He nodded.

"Good. Now, let's join hands, remembering to balance each other. Imagine that I'm pushing against you, and you're pulling me. Be gentle but firm." When she settled her warm palm against his, he fought the urge to close his eyes. Never had such a seemingly benign thing as simply touching a woman hit with a more erotic jolt.

Music throbbed all around them, inside him, and when she urged her hips forward, indicating that it was time for them to begin, the feeling was tantamount to him laying her on a sofa and drawing her into a kiss. Each step brought her breasts against his chest.

She was so tempting.

He was so damn hungry.

Since meeting her, he had done nothing but replay their hours together. He would be in the middle of an important meeting and swear he'd heard her laugh or caught a whiff of her exotic perfume. Had she cast a spell on him? Bankers weren't supposed to long for passionate, artistic women.

"You're doing much better," Rose said, her breath hot against the base of his throat. "I'm glad you haven't forgotten."

Forgotten, hell. Round about last Tuesday, he'd started a secret collection of tango's greatest hits. He listened to them in the car, in the shower, even at his office when there was no one else around. If he was dancing better tonight, then it was because he'd done as she'd initially asked and let the music inside of him.

When the song ended, Rose pulled away. "Wonderful. That was great." The next song began, but she walked to the stereo to press Pause. "Someone did his homework."

"It shows?"

"Definitely. I told you absorbing the music would help you get a better feel for the dance and look, already, your inborn sense of rhythm has improved, which means…"

We're finished? I no longer have to pretend I don't want to pull you into my arms and kiss you like there's no tomorrow?

"…we can start learning individual steps."

"Swell."

And so Dalton spent the better part of two hours pretending he was at the Hot Pepper Dance Academy solely to dance. He pretended not to be mesmerized by Rose's perfume or the way she laughed at his pathetic jokes or lifted her hair and fanned the nape of her neck when she'd grown too warm. If there was one thing all his years in business had taught him, it was how to keep a poker face.

A few minutes past nine, she said, "That'll do for tonight."

"Good. I felt like I was beginning to get sloppy." *The effort of keeping up the charade that this is just a dance and you're just a woman is getting old.*

"No," she reassured. "You're only tired. Which is understandable. I'm amazed by how much you've improved. Not just your footwork, but your concentration." Washing her fingertips over his forehead and cheeks caused a wave of emotion to swell in his belly. "You seemed so focused."

"That a bad thing?"

Knowing if she touched him even a fraction of a second longer, he'd lose the few remnants of his control, he backed away.

"Not at all. In fact, it's quite good. That is, assuming you're not focusing so hard on your lessons in the hopes of getting them over with."

There she went again, reading his mind.

"Because if that is the case, you need to rethink your strategy."

"But if my dancing's better, what does it matter how it got that way?"

A frown marred her mouth's usually serene lines. "Because, you big lug, haven't you heard a word I've been saying? To truly learn tango, you've got to learn to listen to your own body. Yes, I can teach you the steps, but the rhythm, the mood, the feeling, that all has to come from here…" She placed her open hand over his stumbling heart, then smiled. "Ahhh, good. There's something going on in there."

This was insanity.

Being here with Rose, talking about such nonsense as his beating heart. He couldn't do it. The truth was, it hurt too bad. Created longings in him he'd thought were long buried. Longings for a different sort of life.

"Look," he said, "I don't mean to be blunt, but I'm paying for a few simple lessons, and that's all I want." When he spun away, her hand naturally fell, and his heart beat once again. Cold, but sure and steady, just the way it was supposed to.

"Dalton?" she asked, voice floating as if through a dream.

"Yes?" he said without looking back.

"It's happening, isn't it?"

"What?" His hand was on the door. All he had to do to escape was twist the knob and push.

"The dance. It's changing you. Working its magic."

Open the door, man. Set yourself free. "I—I don't know what you're talking about."

"Want to come upstairs for a snack while I explain?"

Yes. "No. Maybe some other time."

His hand was on the door.

He was almost home free.

So why did he feel more like he was stepping into a self-imposed prison than freedom? Why did he feel as if all of the choice had drained from his life until only duty and obligation remained? And truthfully Carly had damn near destroyed him, and he never wanted to hurt that way again.

"Goodbye, Dalton. Will you call to set up your next lesson?"

"Sure."

"Good. Drive safely."

Watching Dalton walk out the door was harder than Rose had imagined. She wanted to run after him, apologize for spouting all that emotional stuff. Had her babble been what chased him away?

She didn't want to get attached, but if letting go was the right thing, how come seeing him actually leave felt so bad?

Rose rested her forehead against the cool glass of the door Dalton had just strode through, wishing with everything in her that she could find some small piece of the professionalism she'd once clung to so confidently.

"NEXT ON THE AGENDA," Alice Craigmoore said in Duffy's back room, "is the Miss Hot Pepper Pageant. Mona, are you ready with your report?"

As was his habit at this portion of the meeting, Dalton took this as a cue to zone out. Legs outstretched under the table, he arched his head back and closed his eyes.

Mona cleared her throat. "Not so fast, lover boy. You might want to stay awake for the next few minutes."

"Why's that?" he asked, cracking one eye open, ignoring what he assumed was a not-so-subtle reference to the amount of time he'd been spending with Rose.

She took a manila folder from her red satchel, then scooted it across the table, nearly dumping his Coke.

"What is it?" he asked, eyeing it as if it were the bill for their meals.

"Alice mentioned seeing you with your new dance instructor, Rose, at the park."

"And?" He straightened, already reaching into his suit pocket for a chewable antacid. This couldn't be good.

"And…" Alice said, leaning forward on the table, "I think she's adorable. My best friend, Gail, from needle-point club sends her granddaughter to the dance academy for jazz and tap. Well, that got me to thinking, why not *jazz* up our usual show by adding another number? Since you've been working so hard we'll, of course, keep your solo, but once I asked around town as to the matter of Rose's credentials and discovered that—"

"Hey," Mona complained. "I thought I was in charge of this issue?"

"Oh, you are, dear. But naturally, as the current chamber president, what with Ms. Vasquez's impressive background, I would think she'd be most comfortable working with someone of my stature."

"*Your* stature?" Mona leaped to her feet. Hands on her hips, face blotchy and red, she said, "How dare you act all high and mighty like this with me, Alice Craigmoore. Which of us was homecoming queen and who wasn't even in *my* royal court? Whose *two* daughters were crowned Miss Hot Pepper?"

Not to be outdone, Alice was on her feet, as well. "While we're strolling memory lane, Mona, whose father donated the Caddie convertible that the homecoming queen and her court rode in? Everyone knows that's the only reason you won."

"That's it." Mona snatched up her folder, shoving it into her satchel. "I've put up with your condescending attitude for decades, Alice Craigmoore, but never again. As of this moment, I resign."

"You can't resign," Alice said. "You're the only one who's familiar with the pageant."

"What's that?" Mona asked, free hand to her ear. "Did someone actually admit I know a little something?"

"Ladies, ladies," Frank said, "both of you should calm down. How about we order a nice round of cobbler à la mode—my treat—and talk this out like the civilized business leaders we are?"

"Hush!" both women said in unison to Frank.

"I'm out of here." Dalton pushed back his chair. "If any of you need me, you know where I'll be."

"Wait just a doggone minute," Frank said. "I'm not stayin' here on my own with these two."

"Looks like the matter's already been taken out of your hands." Dalton nodded toward their fellow committee members, who'd just flown the coop.

Mona left, too.

Then Alice.

"Now what?" Frank asked.

"Beats me," Dalton said.

"Well, clearly, we can't let the pageant be canceled."

Sounds like an excellent plan to me. "Frank, come on, be reasonable. We're just two guys here, what could we possibly know about planning a pageant?"

"Together? Nothing. But I've got a wife, and word has it you and this dance teacher of yours are sweet on each other. Think she might want to help?"

Dalton groaned.

"Mommy?"

"Yes, ma'am?" In the utility room, Rose glanced her daughter's way. They were doing laundry and, as Anna wore more of the still-warm-from-the-dryer navy towels than she'd folded, she clearly needed more lessons on dryer duty.

"Do I make a pretty, deep-sea princess?"

"You're gorgeous, baby." Rose blew her daughter a kiss.

"I'm not a baby."

"Oh—right. Sorry, I forgot how much you've grown in the past week."

"Yep, and Mrs. Clayton says that—"

Ding-dong.

"Hold that thought," Rose said with a tweak to the little girl's nose. "I'll be right back."

Jogging to the loft's back-porch entrance, she peeked past lacy curtains, then willed her pulse to slow.

I am not excited to see him.

I am not excited to see him.

Yeah, right. Rose tossed open the door. "Dalton. Hi."

"Hey. Sorry to just drop in like this, but—"

"Hi, Mr. Dalton!" Anna rushed his way. "Mommy and me are playing sea princess. Wanna come watch?"

"Love to," he said, sharing a grin with Rose.

"Come on," Anna said, taking his hand. "We've got lots of towels. I'll make you a cape!"

Thirty minutes later, Rose was still smiling while poor, sweet Dalton had been made sea king with a tinfoil crown. Finally, Anna tired of being a princess and moved on to her Barbies.

"Thanks," Rose said. "John used to hang out with her all the time. She misses him a lot."

"It was my pleasure." He smiled. "She's a doll."

"You're one, too," Rose claimed, kissing his cheek. "Stay for dinner?"

"Thought you'd never ask."

"I have a sort of favor to ask," he said while she took pork chops from the freezer, "that's the reason I'm here."

"Name it." She popped the meat into the microwave to thaw.

"Love to." He scratched his head. "Trouble is, I'm not even sure what I need you to do." He explained about Alice and Mona's feud, and how everyone else had walked out, too, leaving him and Frank in charge.

"I've judged tons of pageants. A small-scale one like this shouldn't be too much trouble, especially since Mona has probably already done most of the legwork."

"That's a relief."

"Green beans or broccoli?"

"Broccoli. You know how to make cheese sauce?"

"Colby jack or cheddar?"

"Woman—" clutching his chest, his lips curved into a dead-sexy grin "—I'm not sure what I did to warrant you coming into my life, but whatever it was, I need to keep it up."

"Er, thanks. I think."

"Make no mistake, you're a very good thing." Before she had time to process that, he asked, "What can I do to help?"

Chapter Seven

"I want another one!" Anna demanded after Rose had finished her first bedtime story.

"Nope. You've got school in the morning, and it's already fifteen minutes past your bedtime."

"Mmmph…" Pouting, she crossed her arms beneath her pink comforter. "Daddy would've let me stay up."

Even from where Dalton stood in the shadowy corner at Anna's request, so he, too, could hear her story, he saw the pain in Rose's eyes.

"He probably would have let you stay up," Rose said, voice remarkably calm, "but he's not here, and I am, and I say go to sleep."

When Anna pulled the cover over her head, Rose just kissed her head—or at least what she must have thought was her daughter's head—through the downy blanket. "Good night. I love you."

"Mmmph…"

Rose gestured for him to precede her out of the room.

"Night, kiddo," Dalton called over his shoulder.

Out popped a fuzzy-haired head. "Good night, Mr. Dalton."

Sighing, Rose pulled Anna's bedroom door shut. "The joys of being a single mom."

"Do you get grief like this often?"

"Not all that much," she said, aiming for the kitchen. "Mostly just when she doesn't get her way. She has her father's iron will."

"That a good or bad thing?" Dalton asked, taking a seat on an orange-cushioned bar stool.

"Depends on what kind of day I've had." She took a chilled bottle of red wine from the fridge, giving it an enticing wag. "Want some?"

"Absolutely. That scene has me worried about the time when I finally have my own kids."

"Oh, stop." She poured wine into two tall-stemmed glasses. "I wouldn't trade her for anything. Yes, she's occasionally a handful, but for the most part, she's also my best friend. I adore her."

"That's plain to see. And aside from the sass, the way she emulated you while we were cooking, it's also obvious she adores you."

"I hope so," she said, taking a sip of wine. "Lots of times I wonder if I'll be enough for her."

"You could remarry. Give her a stepdad."

"That a proposal?" she asked with a wink.

While he laughed on the outside, inside, Dalton's heart lurched at the notion that living out the rest of his life with a vibrant woman like Rose and her firecracker of a daughter would be amazing. Too bad he'd already determined she wasn't the right type of woman for him.

"Seriously," she said, "in the hospital, after the accident, John told me to be happy. Marry again and have more babies if that was what I wanted. But when you're blessed with a love like ours, I don't know…" She shrugged, sipped her wine. "Sorry. I didn't mean for the conversation to get this heavy."

"It's fine," he said. *You're fine.* In so many ways. Each day, he found himself more enthralled with her laugh, her dancing, her cooking, parenting. "In fact, I'm honored you consider me enough of a friend to confide in me like this."

"Is that what we are?" she asked after taking another sip. "Friends?"

"Well, sure. We both lead pretty full lives. I just assumed that with you, anyway, friendship is all you'd have room for."

"And if I did have room for more?"

Holy crap. What was she saying? Why did his heart feel near bursting with hope? He'd long since established she was all wrong for him, so why was it the more he was with her, the more everything about her felt right?

Retreating to the living area, she said, "That was incredibly presumptuous of me. I'm tired and babbling and—"

"Hush." In a few steps, he went to her. Took her wineglass and set it on the coffee table.

"I mean, listen to me. You're probably not even attracted to me, and Lord knows, I'm trying not to be attracted to you. I don't even know what made me say something like that, other than—"

Cradling her face with his hands, Dalton silenced her sweet objections in the surest way he knew. His kiss was no doubt bumbling and oafish, but judging by the way she clung to him, she didn't care.

"Look at me," she said when he pulled back, "I'm trembling."

"That bad?"

"That good. Only—" Tears welling, she shook her head.

"What?"

"Nothing."

"Please, Rose, don't do this to me. Don't shut me out. Is this about John?"

With a sniffle, she nodded.

"This was your first kiss since him, wasn't it? I mean, your first *real* kiss."

"Yes. And it was beautiful. And the excitement swelling in my chest is almost more than I can bear. But at the same time, there's this guilt. Why am I here and he isn't? Have I mourned enough to properly respect the love we shared? Is he looking down on me? If so, does he approve? Then there's the fear. I loved him so much. What if I end up giving my heart to you, then something happens, and…" Glistening eyes turned to full-on tears.

"Shh…" Dalton said, pulling her against him, smoothing her hair. "It's okay. Everything's going to be okay."

"You don't know that. Seriously, I could fall for you, and Anna could fall for you, and then you could die. And listen to me, I've already got you married with a child and we haven't even been on an official first date. I'm certifiable."

"Honey, trust me, you're not alone in having demons. Do you think my life's perfect?"

"Of course not. No one's is."

Drawing her to the sofa, he gingerly sat her down, handed her her wine, then snagged a paper towel from the holder on the bar. "Blow your nose."

Taking the rough square, she did as he'd asked, and never had Dalton seen a woman look prettier. Not that he got his kicks from watching women cry, just that there was something profoundly intimate in the experience they'd just shared.

He took a deep drink of his wine, then he set it on a side table, pulling her snug against him. "When I was a kid, my dad used to take me to the bank with him Saturday mornings. He had this whole junior-executive station set up in a corner of his office. Toy adding machine and money and a hat that said Banker across the front. I used to love being with him. Having him show me off to his friends, tell everyone that one day, running the bank would be my responsibility. I used to be so damn proud of this fact. You know, most of my friends didn't graduate high school having a clue who or what they wanted to be, but here I had my whole life charted. What Dad didn't instill in me businesswise,

Mom did, giving pointers on the right sort of woman to marry. She must be strong, yet supportive. Independent, yet not so independent as to want her own all-consuming career. It'd be best, she always said, to find a woman with homemaking aspirations."

"You're kidding, right?" Rose said with a sputter of wine. "*Homemaking aspirations?* What century were you in at the time?"

"Crazy, huh?"

"That's the polite way of putting it. And here I thought I had issues."

"Told you," he said, leaning in for another kiss. "So anyway, imagine my surprise when I got to college and discovered this whole other world. For once, late-night discussions didn't revolve around money, or whether to send three or four tellers to the state teller convention."

"They have such a thing?"

"Last year's international teller convention was held in Stockholm."

Rose whistled. "Okay, so enough of your brain being expanded while in college. How did you do with the ladies once Mommy and Daddy weren't looking on?"

He laughed. "Let's just say I was a quick learner and leave it at that."

"Mmm… Met up with a few naughty girls, did you? Shame, shame." This time, she leaned in to kiss him. "So which came first, all this wild-girl chasing? Or the sculpting?"

"Actually, around about the first time we had a nude model in figure studies, things started getting fun."

His grin and wink earned him a playful rib jab. "You were a bad boy."

She snuggled deeper against him. "Okay, so tell me what drew you to sculpting. What is there about it that makes your heart feel full?"

"First off, aside from Anna's Play-Doh, I haven't so much as touched a lump of clay in a decade, so I don't even know if it would still be a thrill. All I do know is that back then, something about the connection between my hands and brain and the way I could actually make something of strength and importance and beauty that had nothing to do with numbers, but simply my sheer will to create…" Sharply exhaling, he said, "It was heady stuff."

She didn't say anything. Just sat there, grinning.

"What? I pour out my heart to you and you think it's funny?"

"Dalton, Dalton," she said, voice as refreshing as a margarita. Urging him sideways, she placed her hands on his shoulders and rubbed. "You're tense. Meaning, you've taken my actions in the wrong spirit. I'm smiling because I'm touched by the notion of you having a grand passion outside of the bank. That's a wonderful thing." She deepened her strokes, and he closed his eyes, loving every second of the massage. "You've got to learn to relax. Take time out from your busy schedule to smell the roses. Who knows? Maybe your best course of action would be running right out in the morning to purchase a chunk of clay."

He swung around to face her, a look of desperation in his eyes. "Don't you get it? My whole life is mapped out. My dad isn't well and, possibly within the year, that bank and all the people who work there will become my responsibility."

"But, Dalton, you could—"

"It's late," he said with a tender kiss to her forehead. "I should go."

"But shouldn't we talk? You're obviously upset."

"I'm fine. Just not ready to tackle something this big."

"Fair enough. But what if I said I have other reasons for not wanting you to go?"

"Like what?"

"I don't want you to." She rested her head on his shoulder, flooding him with well-being and a consuming urge to protect and comfort and make her fears go away.

"I don't want me to, either. But we've both got full days tomorrow."

"I know. I guess I just want to establish what it is we're doing."

"In what sense?"

"I don't know." Hand fisted beneath her chin, she sighed. "You and me. *Us.* All of this is so comfortable and yet foreign."

"Tell you what," he said, tucking her hands into his, "let's just take this one day at a time. No rules or expectations. Just fun."

"Yeah," she said, blindsiding him with a smile that didn't quite reach her eyes. She was such a contradiction. All at once full of life, and yet heartbreaking in her buried sorrow. With everything in him, he wanted to be everything to her. But even he was smart enough to realize he didn't have that kind of power. Moreover, shouldn't *want* that kind of power. "Let's just play."

"Walk me out?"

"Uh-huh."

Dalton stood, offering his hand to help her from the sofa. They walked to the back door in companionable silence. He kissed her forehead. She gave his waist a squeeze, and he left, knowing that no matter what else happened between them, his life was forever changed by Rose Vasquez's smile.

"Aren't you the new owner of Miss Gertrude's?"

Rose glanced up from the paperback she'd been reading at the corner booth of Big Daddy's to see a burly man grinning down at her. "Yes, I'm Rose Vasquez," she said, holding out her hand for him to shake. "And you're…?"

"Frank Loveaux. This is my place and that's my secret raspberry-tea recipe you've now had five glasses of."

"You've been counting?" she asked. Was it time for her to slowly get up, then run?

"Oh—the only reason I even paid attention was because I've been working up my courage to come talk to you."

"Am I that scary?"

"No, no," he said with a brawny laugh that instantly put her at ease. "Just that we've got a bit of a situation brewing on the Miss Hot Pepper Pageant committee, and—"

"Are Mona and Alice still not talking?"

"You've heard about that?"

"Dalton filled me in, and I told him I'd be happy to help with whatever you need."

"When did you talk with him?" Frank asked, easing his large frame into the booth's empty half.

"Last night."

"Did he have a lesson?"

"No."

"Did he call?" Frank helped himself to one of Rose's homemade chips.

Rose eyed him. "Do you mind?"

"Oops. Sorry. Nervous habit." He waved over the waitress to bring more. "Now, where were we?"

"You were in the process of seriously invading my privacy."

"About Dalton, you mean? I just don't understand how he got to you so quickly if you didn't have a lesson. Alice says she thinks y'all are sweet on each other, but I told her that with his dad so ill, Dalton's got his mind on taking care of business."

"I knew his dad had heart trouble, but is it really that serious?"

When the new chips came, Frank helped himself. "I don't gossip, but word around town is that he's got one foot in the grave. 'Course, he's always been ornery as a swarm of hornets, so he's one of those sorts I expect to outlast us all."

"Oh," Rose said, sipping her tea. While she was sorry to hear that Dalton's father truly was gravely ill, it was reassuring to know that Dalton had been telling the truth. Not that she'd doubted him. Or had she? Maybe it was her own feelings she distrusted?

"So which is it?" Frank asked, leaning in extra close. "I can keep a secret. You and Dalton having a wild fling?"

"Mr. Loveaux!" Reaching for her purse, Rose fished out a ten and slapped it on the table.

"Sorry, sorry. Didn't mean to offend. It's just that if Mona and Alice don't soon make amends, I'm not sure what we're going to do."

"Mr. Loveaux, I've already said I don't mind helping. And for the record, Dalton and I are not *sweet* on each other, merely friends."

"Of course. Again, sorry, sorry." The man shot her a flamboyant wave. "Usually when Alice says something, you can take it as gospel, but duly noted that in this case, she was wrong."

During the walk back to her studio, Rose tried focusing on the beautiful spring day. On the historic, weathered brick storefronts, the red and yellow tulips lining the brick sidewalk and sounds of giggling kindergartners walking in a row on their field trip to the fire station. Anna's first-grade class would be going soon, too. Rose tried focusing on all of that, but instead, the only thing she could think about was her speedy denial of her and Dalton's relationship.

For heaven's sake, she'd spent a large portion of last night kissing the man, pouring out her soul to him, admiring his gorgeous face and broad shoulders and knack for making her little girl smile. If all of that didn't add up to at the very least a serious crush, she wasn't sure what did. What was she so afraid of? Why couldn't she—

"Hi, Miss Rose!" Samantha, from her Tuesday-night ballet class, waved from her spot in the line of kindergartners.

"Hey, sweetie. Having a good time?"

"Uh-huh! We're going to pet the firemen's Dalmatian."

"Mmm… Sounds fun." She patted the girl's back. "Give him a hug from me."

"Okay."

Rose should've felt uplifted by the fact that she and her dance academy were getting established enough in the community that in taking a simple walk down the street, she'd encountered one of her students. But even that did nothing to lighten the dull ache in her heart.

Why?

Because, as she'd told him, falling for Dalton was potentially risky. Not just for herself, but Anna. What if they both gave of themselves heart and soul to him, only to have something tragic happen again? Would they survive the pain? Was she being a responsible parent in considering entering another serious relationship? On the flip side, why did anything about what she and Dalton shared have to be serious?

They were adults. What were a few fun kisses between friends?

Trouble was, the more she was around Dalton, the more her heart trilled at just the sight of him, the more she realized her burning fascination with him was starting to be a problem.

She had a little girl and a growing dance studio needing her attention.

Dalton had a bank to run.

So where did that leave them?

Rose was heartily confused, but unwilling to hide from the issue. If there was one thing losing her husband at such a young age, then single-handedly raising their daughter, had taught her, it was to fight for what she wanted. And truthfully, in a secret, lonely corner of her heart, she very much wanted a confidant, friend and possibly even lover in Dalton Montgomery.

Chapter Eight

"You again?" the bank lobby's boyish, redheaded guard dog asked when Rose marched by later in the afternoon.

"Excuse me?" she said, caught off guard by the man's rather rude greeting.

"Sorry, it's just that I got in trouble for letting you wander through the executive wing. No one's supposed to be up there except people who have appointments."

"Oh," she said, continuing toward the lobby stairs.

"Do you?" he asked, doggedly trailing after her.

"Do I what?" she asked with an innocent smile.

"Have an appointment?"

"Of course."

"With who?" he probed, while she shifted her heavy package from the crook of her right arm to her left and kept right on marching up the stairs.

"Dalton Montgomery."

"I'm pretty sure he's in a meeting."

"I'm pretty sure—"

"Bradley, let me handle this." Dalton, looking incredibly sexy in a black suit and cobalt shirt that matched his eyes, strode across the sea of navy carpet. Her pulse raced. "Are you ever a sight for sore eyes."

Ditto.

"Thank you," she said while he proprietarily slipped his hand around her waist, drawing her into his office, then shutting the door. "You're looking pretty good yourself."

She adjusted his tie, flicked a bit of lint from his left lapel.

While Dalton struggled for something appropriately witty to say, Rose flashed that smile of hers that always managed to turn his heart upside down. Calmly setting her brown paper bag on his desk before taking a seat in his chair, she spun a couple times before landing her feet square in the middle of his latest file. Her silky red dress slid high on her thighs as she raised her hands to sweep her hair back from her forehead.

Just looking at her stole his every thought.

Did she have any idea what her being here did to him?

His whole life had been about carefully compartmentalizing his emotions, but from the second she'd walked through his office door, his safety net had hung in tatters.

"What's wrong?" she asked, crossing her arms beneath her breasts, unwittingly deepening her cleavage by a tantalizing inch. "Your complexion looks pasty." She touched her forehead. "And your frown is back."

"I feel tired. You shouldn't be here."

"How come?"

"Because you're bad for my concentration."

"When you admittedly don't much care for your work," she teased, "I fail to see how my distracting you is a bad thing."

"I'm the boss," he said, taking hold of her slim ankles. "My being distracted is potentially bad for business." Not to mention his failing willpower. His hand on her left calf, he eased it up past her knee, not stopping until he reached the back of her thigh.

She swallowed hard. "Looks like you're in total control to me." Wriggling free of his hold to rest her feet primly on the floor, she nodded to the bag. "Aren't you going to open your present?"

"Why? When I have a pretty good guess what's inside."

"You're no fun," she said with a playful pout.

Oh, but the sight of her made him want to be.

"Okay, so you guessed I bought you a chunk of clay. Maybe the real question of the day is what are you going to do with it."

"Not a bloody thing," he said with regret, grasping her hands to pull her out of his chair. "I've got meetings stacked like jumbo jets waiting to land. I've got letters to dictate and contracts to sign. I've got—"

She pressed her fingers to his lips, her body to his. "What you've got," she said, her voice a throaty whisper, "is a woman who wants to spend the day with you." Fisting his starched shirt, she pulled him excruciatingly close before planting a warm, juicy, delectably sweet kiss to his lips.

Through a groan, he said, "I can't do this…."

"Try," she said, deepening the kiss, deepening his internal struggle. He wanted this—her—so damn bad, but he was due in Alice's office in two minutes. "You've got too many clothes on," she said, sliding nimble fingers between the buttons on his shirt, only to encounter a T-shirt.

"And I mean to keep them on."

"Not if I can help it." She flashed her sexiest grin, telling him loud and clear that he was lost. She'd somehow, some way, taken him hostage.

"Why are you doing this? What about everything we talked about last night?" Sliding his fingers under the fall of her hair, he demanded, "Taking things slow?"

"Just for today," she said, kissing him senseless, "make me forget the heartache. Anna's at school, then going straight to soccer. The dance academy's closed till later. Come with me to the loft. We'll be all alone. Just you and me and your clay."

Eyes closed, he drew her close. "You don't know how tempting that sounds."

The intercom on his desk buzzed. "Dalton?"

"Yes?"

The object of his every desire slowly backed toward the door, temptingly crooking her index finger, beckoning him to take a walk on the wild side.

Joan, his secretary, said, "Mr. Rossdale from Fontaine Industries is on line one. He doesn't sound happy about the rating you gave their stock."

"Come with me," Rose whispered. "Make me happy. Make *you* happy."

"I can't," Dalton whispered back.

"Excuse me?" Joan said. "Shall I tell him you're in a meeting?"

"No—yes." Dear God, what was he doing? "Tell everyone I'm out for the day."

"Um, okay. Shall I tell folks why?"

"I'm sick." Lovesick. Heartsick. Crazed in the head. It didn't matter what the malaise was. All that truly mattered was that the cure stood smiling before him.

"How's THIS?" Rose asked, striking a pose before floor-to-ceiling windows. Late-afternoon sun warmed her face and throat and she instinctively let her white robe fall lower on her shoulders.

Dalton's happy grunt told her all she needed to know. Her plan to lure him from his office and into his passion was working, as was her attempt to, for just one afternoon, forget she was a widow and single mom and focus on being a woman.

Dalton had only been at the loft a couple hours, but already, his sculpture of her was taking shape. The brick-size chunks of clay she'd gifted him with at his office had only been for play. Back at her loft, she'd called in a favor from her friend Hector, who ran an art-supply store in a neighboring town to deliver two twenty-five-pound bags of moist, red clay that Dalton was now molding and shaping around a wire frame.

"I've never seen you look so relaxed," she said, arching her head into a more comfortable position.

He chuckled, misting the clay with water. "I can't remember ever feeling more relaxed. I'd forgotten how much fun this is."

"So why don't you do it more often?"

"I was taught that art—unless it's the classical kind sold for millions at auction—is for wusses." Dalton went on to tell her about his father hurling his clay likeness into their living room hearth on the Christmas Dalton told him he didn't want to spend the rest of his life working at the bank.

He left out the part where instead, right out of college, he'd married Carly and started a garage art studio with the proceeds he'd made from selling his new Mustang—a graduation gift from his folks. He'd thought sharing the story—or, at least part of it—would leave him sad, but if anything, retelling it felt cleansing. In a sense, he was exorcising part of his rocky past.

Would it dispel his fear of committing to another creative woman? Who knew? For the moment, all that mattered was Rose's sweet, supportive smile.

Before he could stop her, Rose left her sunny perch to slide between him and his cherished bag of clay. She twined her arms around his neck and gave him the best hug he'd ever had.

"Watch it," he said, holding up his reddish-brown hands. "I'm going to get you all dirty."

"So?" She flashed that mischievous grin he found ever more irresistible. "Maybe I like being dirty."

Reaching behind her, she dredged her index finger through the bag, then drew two red lines across Dalton's cheeks.

"What are you doing?" he asked, looking puzzled.

"Giving you courage." *Hmm... Maybe I need a few lines, too.*

"By drawing on my face?"

"Many Native American tribes believed painting on war faces gave extra strength in battle." She tugged free of his hold, then drew additional lines on his cheeks and chin. "Isn't that what you're engaged in with your father? A battle over how you want to live the rest of your life?"

"I don't know that I'd put it in such dramatic terms." Especially when the real battle was being waged within him.

"Then how would you put it?" Cradling his face in her hands, she nudged herself farther between his legs. "Here we are, both dying to get to know each other, but something's holding you back. If it isn't your father and his dream of you taking over his bank, then what?"

"You don't understand," he said. "It's not as simple as any one thing."

"Then make me understand."

"He recently suffered a massive heart attack. Before, I might've told him how I really feel about carrying on the family tradition, but now…" As his words trailed off, Rose drew his head against her chest. Even though it was barely four, Dalton's faint five o'clock shadow prickled the tops of her breasts, reminding her that however much she wept for the sad little boy inside him, on the outside he was all man.

A man she wanted before she lost her nerve.

Smoothing his hair back from his forehead, she said, "I'm sorry about your dad, Dalton. Truly, I am, but don't you see? You're trading your life for his, and that's not fair to you. Do you think he'd even want you to do that for him?" Strong words from a woman desperately attempting to conquer her own ghost.

Not giving him a chance to answer, she straddled his waist, loving his swift intake of breath when he realized she wore nothing beneath her robe. All that stood between the two of them taking the most intimate plunge a couple can was the thin poly/cotton blend of his slacks. He swelled beneath her, telling her with his body what he couldn't—or wouldn't—say with his mouth.

"Make me forget, Dalton. *Please.*" Tears closed up the back of her throat, but she'd be damned if she'd let them fall. She stopped them with a kiss to end all kisses. Just the crush of their lips was heady enough. But nothing could have prepared her for the stunning jolt of pleasure when she boldly slipped her tongue into his mouth.

After that, nothing else mattered. Right now, here, all she cared about was being as close to Dalton as possible.

Dalton raised his arms while Rose dragged his T-shirt over his head. The moment their lips were apart felt like an eternity, but then she was back, skimming her fingers through his chest hair. Tickling him. Loving him.

He slid clay-slick hands inside her robe, relishing the feel of her silky hot skin. He skimmed his fingers up her rib cage, cupping her full breasts. He teased her nipples, bringing them to life with his tongue, then sucking hard when Rose dug her fingers into the back of his head.

She pulled his hair.

He sucked harder.

She wrenched his belt free, yanking it through the loops before flinging it across the room. It landed with a clatter near her bed, reminding him that that's where this should be happening. He should treat this exquisite creature to the softest round of lovemaking he knew how to give, but his need was too great to stop and suggest a change of venue.

"I want you so bad," she said, working the button, then fly, of his slacks before slipping his boxers free.

He slid his hands to her hips, lifting her, then setting her atop the center of his need.

"Oh…" Rose exclaimed, initially caught off guard, then meeting him thrust for thrust. It'd been so long since she'd been with a man. Part of her wanted to cry out for Dalton to stop, that this was going too fast. She was still confused about so many things. But another part had to free her from the past in the purest way possible.

By loving another.

But did she really love Dalton? Or was she, in a sense, using him?

No. Never. She wasn't that kind of woman.

At least she didn't used to be.

But then there was no more room for thinking, because the mounting pleasure was too intense. All that existed was this man and the unfathomable joy he brought her.

When release finally came, nothing could have prepared her for the shock. She shivered and moaned, leaning backward, then forward, biting Dalton's shoulder to contain her pleasure...

And crushing pain.

What have I done?

She'd wanted so desperately to make love with Dalton to remind herself to live—and for a few mind-blowing minutes, the plan had worked. But now, safe in Dalton's arms, her fears were back. How come as much as she craved being around him, she now wondered if she should run? Every day she was growing more attached to the man, as was her daughter. Love was a wonderful thing, but losing it was horrible. Might she be better off backing away from Dalton now? Before they grew even closer? Before she'd invested her heart, and her daughter's, past the point of no return?

"DALTON, dear," his mother said over soft classical music, "would you please pass the rolls?"

He snagged two more whole wheat crescent rolls for himself before passing the bowl to his mom. At the same dining room table where he'd eaten Sunday lunch for the vast majority of his life, he'd become an outsider. The white linen napkins, gleaming cherry table and crystal and silver felt foreign.

He would've felt more at home using the chunky, brightly colored plates he'd eaten off of at Rose's. He missed the vibrant Latin music and Anna's incessant chatter. Most of all, he missed Rose. Her throaty laugh, her musky scent and the way she—

"So, son," his dad said, "I heard that on Thursday you went home sick. *With* your dance teacher. That true?"

"Yes."

"You were supposed to preside over the Fontaine matter."

"I rescheduled for Monday."

"Now, son," his dad said, scowl presumably deepened by his latest forkful of his heart-friendly, dry-as-a-bone baked potato. "I don't mean to get in your business, but—"

"Dad, I took one afternoon off. No one died. The bank's walls didn't shatter around me."

"Don't you mock me," his dad thundered.

"William," his mom warned, resting her pale hand on his father's forearm, "you know what the doctor said about losing your temper."

"I'm not losing my temper. I'm merely ensuring the one person charged with carrying on my legacy understands the whole point of his having an office at the bank is so that he can actually be at the bank."

"I think Dalton knows that, dear." His mom was back to patting. "You need to calm down. Practice your meditation techniques."

"I don't need to meditate, dammit, I need to know the

boy isn't going to foul up the institution my father and his father spent their lifetimes building. And for that matter, when are you starting your own family? Miranda Browning's not getting any younger."

"First off," Dalton said, tone deliberately low and in control, "I'm no longer a boy, but a man, and Miranda and I are just friends. Second, under my direction, *your* institution is doing fine. It's posted record profits for the past two quarters. Customer satisfaction and loyalty are also at all-time highs. Fifteen new branches have been added in Polk and Hampstead Parishes, while—"

"That's all well and good," his dad raged at full volume, "but you can't rest on your laurels. You have to be there. Let your employees know who's in control."

Looks like you're in total control to me.

Dalton held back a grin at the memory of Rose's words that day in his office when she hadn't had to work very hard to convince him to play hooky. "I think they know, Dad."

"They know, William," his mother reassured.

His dad's only reaction was a grunt.

"Whew, that was perfect," Rose said, crossing the studio to change CDs. She had expected being back in Dalton's arms for the first time after they'd made love to feel strained, but to the contrary, it was exhilarating fun. A fine sheen of moisture coating her chest, she lingered at the stereo to pat herself with a towel.

"You really think I'm improving?" Dalton asked.

"Are you nuts? You can't feel the change?"

"I guess so, but I thought the difference had more to do with the way I feel about you than my dancing."

She wagged her index finger. "But that's what I've been trying to tell you. So much of tango is feeling. You know enough of the base steps that your confidence is up. You've learned to improvise and be a strong enough leader to allow me freedom of movement. Believe me, I'm highly impressed." Not to mention, turned-on. Yes, after they'd been together, she'd feared the union had been a mistake, but a week's distance had her wanting him more. While her brain told her she should back off, her heart told her to live. Laugh. Love. Which was why with Anna at a slumber party for the night, Rose had decided to teach Dalton a few subtleties of the dance.

"So?" he asked, taking a bottled water from the fridge. "What's next?"

"I have a surprise for you."

"Oh, yeah?"

"Wait here." She dashed out of the studio, then turned off the lobby lights and locked the front door. She drew the shades, then went to the utility closet where she'd stashed candles, some of which she lit before floating them in the fountain. Others, she nested among the plants.

"What's taking so long?" Dalton called from the studio.

"You'll see. Just a few more minutes." Next, she unearthed a sterling wine cooler that her grandmother had given her as a wedding gift. Inside, chilling on ice, was a bottle of pricey champagne. She popped the top and giggled while slurping the foam.

"Will it be worth the wait?"

"Depends. What do you consider worthy?"

He made a strangling sound. "You're kidding, right?"

She dashed back into the studio to tease him with a deep, champagne-flavored kiss. "Did that feel like a joke?"

"Damn," he said with a slow, sexy smile. "What are you trying to do to me?"

"Patience, and you'll find out."

Back in the lobby, Rose plugged in a portable stereo, then switched the CD to *Lo que vendrà,* one of her favorite sultry tangos. John hadn't liked it, which made it all the more perfect for tonight.

All she had to do now was change into the red-hot, curve-hugging dress she had hanging in her office. Once that was accomplished, she raced back to the lobby and smoothed her hair before calling in what she hoped was an appropriately sultry tone, "Come and get me…if you dare."

Dalton, all smiles, clutched his chest. Was his heart strong enough to take whatever this siren had planned? Deciding to risk it, he stepped out of the brightly lit studio and into another world.

Chapter Nine

"Turn out the lights after you, please."

Dalton did as Rose had asked, transforming the room into a shadowy courtyard in old-town Buenos Aires. The candles she'd lit smelled of orchids, but the loveliest flower of all was Rose. She'd changed into a siren's dress that plunged down her chest and back, showcasing her hourglass figure to such a degree that for the first time in his life, Dalton found himself speechless.

"Thirsty?" she asked, sauntering his way with two champagne flutes. All he could do was grin and nod. "You okay?"

"Give me a second. This whole setup is a shock."

"A second, but that's all. I have a full evening planned for you."

Taking the glass she held out for him, he said, "Trust me, I'm all yours."

"Good. Now that that's settled, let's toast." Glass raised, she said, "To moonlight, to lovers everywhere, and most of all, to tango."

"To tango."

They chinked crystal rims, then drank. The champagne was excellent, light and fruity, but far from taking Dalton's mind off of his problems, it brought them more sharply into focus. Though she'd denied it, after they'd made love, he could've sworn he'd heard Rose crying in the bathroom.

Then there were his own issues.

"Hey," his Rose said. And in that moment, she was. *His.* She touched his forehead. "No frowning allowed."

He cupped her cheek, trailing the pad of his thumb along her brow. "You're so beautiful."

"Thank you."

"I've never met anyone like you." Which was true. For the few similarities between Rose and Carly, there were a hundred differences. Improvements. Did he dare trust they were enough to make all the difference in forging a relationship that would last?

"I hope that's a good thing."

"Very." He took her glass and his, setting them on the reception desk.

Though the soft music playing was a tango, he pulled her close, dancing American style, which meant hardly dancing at all, but swaying, savoring her warm curves.

"As wonderful as dancing with you like this is," she said at the song break, "I'm supposed to be teaching you more steps."

"But I like this one."

Grinning, she pulled back. "I do, too, but after all, you have paid me for tango lessons, so I feel honor-bound to share my knowledge."

"In that case, share away."

"All right, tonight's lesson is on the fine art of the glance."

"Excuse me?"

"You know. The glance. Now, in America, it may be fine to walk right up to a woman and ask her to dance, but in many other parts of the world, they use a far more subtle method. Eye contact."

"You've got my attention."

"Good. Now, pretend we've never met."

"Wait a minute. That doesn't sound like fun."

"Humor me." She crossed the room to back onto the low reception desk. Legs crossed, showing an unfair amount of thigh, she said, "Okay, do you hunger?"

"Like a dieter for lasagna."

Laughter sparkling in her eyes, she shook her head. "My sweet Dalton, what am I going to do with you? This is not the time for jokes, but passion. Look at me. *Really* look at me. Let me feel your desire."

Trying to calm his pulse, he asked, "You're presumably teaching me to dance in any setting, right?"

"Of course."

"What if someday, instead of dancing in a beauty pageant, I'm at a South American conference and to be polite, ask an associate's grandmother to step into my arms? Do I really want her *feeling my desire?*"

"I'm pretending you didn't ask that. Every woman, regardless of her age or station, longs to feel desired."

Dalton grinned. "Thinking back, just the other day I did charm the lovely widow Baker into trusting us with her extensive financial holdings. Who knows?" he said, puffing out his chest, "now that I've honed my skills, maybe I can get all of her bridge buddies to give me their business, as well."

"What kind of monster have I created?"

"If you're lucky, you might find out."

Arms crossed, rolling her eyes, she said, "Back to our lesson, you have to make your partner feel cherished and adored. Make her…"

During her scolding, Dalton had crossed the room. Rose wanted to feel cherished and adored, did she? He fixed her with that concentrated stare she'd requested, then traced a path down her shoulder. When she shivered despite the room's growing heat, he figured he was on the right path.

"That's good," she said, voice breathy. "I think you're getting the hang of it. But please don't try anything like that on sweet Mrs. Baker. I don't think her heart can take it."

"Can yours?" He dipped his head to kiss her, but just when their lips touched, he pulled back.

"That's not fair."

"And you wearing that dress is?" As the music intensified, he kissed the base of her throat, then moved on to her neck.

"If you object that strongly, I can cover it with a baggy sweater."

"Don't bother," he said, nibbling her earlobe. "Where you're concerned, inequality's not so hard to take."

"Yes, but—" she sucked in a deep breath when he slid his hand along her inner thigh "—what about fairness to me?"

"Believe me, honey, neither of us will be leaving this room until all issues are addressed," Dalton assured her. To seal that promise, he gave her the kiss he'd previously denied. Starting out soft, mingling their breath before pressing his lips fully to hers. He tasted the champagne on her tongue, sucking her lower lip, running his hands through her hair.

If he were a wise man, he'd back away now. He'd remind himself that even though it was Friday night, he still had to be at his office bright and early in the morning. More important, Rose might come across as a strong, available woman, but with the ghost of her husband still in her heart, she was anything but strong.

She was an amazing person, and as such, deserved more than he could comfortably offer. Sure, he wanted very much to marry one day. He longed to start that family of his own his parents were always nagging him about, but was this really the time? Was Rose really the woman?

"I WON'T DO IT." As the exclamation on the end of her declaration, Mona slammed a box of penny loafers on the shoe store's checkout counter. "That woman's not civilized."

Rose nibbled her pinkie, not for the first time wondering how she'd let herself be talked into trying to ease tensions between Mona and Alice. But then, she hadn't had to be convinced, she'd volunteered. Thankfully, on a Monday morning, the store was still empty, which would hopefully leave plenty of time for her to plead her case. "Seeing how I hardly know either of you, I don't feel qualified to judge Alice's character."

"Then why are you here?"

"To hopefully appeal to your sense of civic pride. Dalton says—"

"I should've guessed. He's behind this, isn't he? He never did want to be on the pageant committee, and once he found out it was his year to dance while the judges tally, he pitched a full-blown fit."

"Yes, well—"

"If anyone needs a lecture about civic duty, I think it's him."

"Mona, trust me, Dalton, more than anyone I've ever known, is familiar with the concept of duty. Now, the way I see it, this pageant has to be planned. Are you willing to put aside whatever petty differences you and Alice have in order to put on the best pageant Hot Pepper has ever seen?"

"Who fed you a happy pill?"

Rose chose to ignore that remark.

"Look," Mona said, stepping out from behind the

counter to straighten the sale rack, "I don't mean to sound unneighborly, but you've been in town only a few months, right?"

"Yes."

"Well, that hardly gives you the right to go poking your nose into town affairs. You're not even a chamber member."

"I own a business. Doesn't that give me the right to join?"

"Well, yes, but—"

"And as a downtown business owner, don't I have just as much at stake in seeing the festival and pageant be a continued success as anyone else in Hot Pepper?"

"Well, yes, but—"

"Never mind," Rose said. "I see why Alice prefers not working with you."

"Wait just a doggone minute. Everyone knows I'm the more reasonable of the two of us. Besides which, most everything is done, save for the awarding of the crown. Oh—and I was going to ask you about putting on an exhibition of sorts with some of your younger students. We—I mean, *I*—thought it would be darling to see your junior dancers do a number. You know, sort of a warm-up to Dalton's grand finale with the outgoing queen. For that matter, you and Dalton can do a number, as well."

"That's a great idea," Rose said. "I think that'll be a lot of fun for the little girls in the audience, dreaming of their own turn to be in the pageant." *And I'll get to spend more time in Dalton's arms.*

"That's exactly what I told Alice."

"So then Frank and Dalton can count on you to handle the pageant from here on out, and I'll tackle the exhibition planning?"

"As long as I don't have to see Alice, I'll be happy to do all I can to help."

"LET ME GUESS," Dalton said in Rose's kitchen, up to his elbows in soap suds while doing dinner dishes from Rose's roasted chicken and scalloped potatoes. "Later, when you spoke with Alice, she took credit for everything, then said she'll be happy to keep pageant preparations moving forward as long as Mona isn't involved."

"You do read minds," Rose said, voice laced with sarcasm while drying the plate he'd handed her.

"Mommy," Anna asked, bounding into the kitchen, skidding the last four feet on her duck slippers, "can Mr. Dalton read my bedtime story?"

"If it's okay with him."

"Fine by me, as long as it's not a girlie story." He made a face. "No rainbows or bunnies. I'm allergic."

Hands on her hips, the girl raised her chin. "You can't be allergic to bunnies. Everybody loves bunnies."

The argument lasted through *Cinderella,* then *Beauty and the Beast,* after which, Anna took a purple bunny from the pile of stuffed animals sharing her bed and kissed Dalton with it.

Squealing with glee, she said, "See? You didn't die, or anything."

"Thank goodness," he said. "I'm so glad I took my antibunny medicine this morning."

"I guess I'm glad, too," she said, wrapping him in a surprise hug. "My daddy died."

"I know. I'm sorry. You must miss him a lot."

"I do. But Mommy misses him more. She never sleeps. And sometimes I hear her crying."

"What do you do when that happens?"

"I used to get up and give her hugs, but now I think she gets all secret mad at me because she likes pretending she's not sad so I won't be sad."

Heart aching for the two of them, Dalton asked, "How does that make you feel?"

"Sad."

"Yeah. Me, too."

"She cried bunches last night."

"You sure it was last night?"

"Uh-huh." Swell. So much for his hope that their love-making would magically cure Rose of her lingering grief.

"Mr. Dalton?"

"Yes?"

"You shouldn't be afraid of bunnies. They're warm and cuddly. I think if you tried holding one, you'd like them."

"Thank you, sweetie. I promise to give bunnies another try."

She yawned. "Okay. Well, I'm going to sleep."

"Sweet dreams," he said, kissing the top of her head.

He left the girl's room and shut the door just as Rose

headed that way. "Already done? The phone rang about two minutes after you started."

"Who was it?"

"Can you believe Alice? She wanted to volunteer her sewing expertise for making costumes."

"Not surprising. Word must have already gotten around that Mona's back on board the pageant train, and Alice didn't want to look bad."

"You think she's that shallow?"

"Eh, she's all right. She does a great job at the bank. She's been there so long, sometimes I think she knows more of what's going on than either Dad or myself." He headed for the kitchen to finish washing up, but he also needed some distance from Rose. His mind was still reeling from Anna's confessions.

"Mona caught me off guard today when she said I had no right worrying about chamber business when I'm not a member."

"Well, that's easy enough to fix." *Unlike the issues making you cry every night.* The knowledge that he wasn't enough for her hit like a punch in the gut. But then, they hadn't even known each other that long. What had he expected? By his own admission, he wasn't anywhere near ready for a commitment. He wasn't her savior, but her friend.

Er, wouldn't that be lover?

Heat rose up his neck.

Good Lord, he should've cooled things off. He should've been strong enough for the both of them.

Trouble was, he was tired of being strong, tired of being noble. Just once more, he longed to throw caution to the wind and—

"You're frowning."

Turning away from her, gripping the counter, he said, "Anna said you cry a lot. Like as recently as last night."

"My daughter talks too much."

"You're denying it?" He turned to face her, and when she looked down, he cupped her chin, forcing her to meet his gaze. "Because if everything's fine with you, now would be a great time to tell me."

Wrenching free of his hold, she escaped to the living area, taking a seat in John's chair. Coincidence? He didn't think so. Especially not when she wrapped her arms around herself in a hug.

"Dammit, Rose…" He went to her, fell to his knees in front of the armchair she'd admitted she kept as a memento of her husband. "If you didn't want to be with me, why the hell didn't you say so?"

"I *do* want to be with you," she said on the heels of a sob. "That's the problem. But part of me wants to be with John, too. It's like he's here," she said, beating her chest, "but not here." She waved to the room. "If he's going to be gone, why won't he just leave? Why can't I be free to live?"

"You can be," he said, brushing at her tears with the pads of his thumbs. "But, honey, not that I'm an expert, but it doesn't happen overnight. If you slept with me, hoping our being together would somehow change things inside of you, I'm thinking you—we—made a serious mistake."

He tugged her forward on the chair, pulling her into his arms. "Let it out, honey. You have to let him go."

"I know," she said, "but I can't."

"Well, I can't compete with a ghost. And truthfully, it hurts like hell knowing the times we were together, you were comparing me to him." *Like you really have room to talk? How many times have you compared Rose to Carly? Assuming that just because she has an artistic career, that she's just as flaky as your first love?*

"It wasn't like that. I like you, Dalton. A lot."

"Just not enough to let him go?"

"It's complicated. Just like you and your dad. I would think of all people, you'd understand."

Coming to his feet, he sighed. "Yes, I should understand, but I don't. I thought we had something here, but—" God, why couldn't he just shut up? He had no right drilling her like this. But he couldn't stop the questions in his heart.

"We do. I just need time to get my head in a good place."

"When will you know?"

"What?"

He laughed sharply, sliced his hands through his hair. "When you've reached that magical place?"

"It isn't like you to be cruel."

"Why do you think you understand me? We barely know each other."

"I know you've spent a lifetime hiding from the man you want to be."

"That's rich. A lecture about hiding, coming from you?"

"Where are you going?" she asked when he headed for the back door.

"What's it look like?"

"You can't just leave like this. Mad. I thought you were going to work on your sculpture?"

"Funny, but I'm just not in the mood."

ALONE, DRIVING DOWN Bayou Road on a moonless night, Dalton knew there was a lot he should be thinking about, but only one thing stuck in his mind. The hollow look in Anna's eyes when she'd talked about her father. He shouldn't be upset with Rose for her loyalty to a man she'd obviously loved. Wouldn't he want the same level of commitment from the woman he someday married?

Trouble was, in Rose's arms he'd toyed with the notion that maybe he had found her. The one and only woman for him. But how could Rose be his when she belonged to another guy?

And what was he supposed to do about the bank? With each passing day he felt more out of control. Not in the sense that the job itself was difficult for him. He could have done it blindfolded. But he resented it like hell. Just pulling his SUV into his assigned spot in the morning left him reaching for antacid. He couldn't go on like this, but he didn't have a clue what he'd rather do.

Yes, sculpting was fun, but so was eating cupcakes, and he sure couldn't support his future family on that.

Next time he saw Rose, maybe he could brainstorm escape plans, alternate careers that might bring him more peace while still paying the electric bill. But after some of the harsh things he'd said to her, would there even be a next time?

Dalton couldn't say for sure whether what he felt for Rose was the real deal or crazy infatuation. One thing he did know was that he couldn't bear the thought of her still crying.

Punching her number into his cell, he prayed she'd answer.

"Dalton?" she asked after the third ring, voice hoarse.

"Good. You're up. I'm on my way."

Chapter Ten

Seeing Dalton's SUV's lights shimmer off the living room wall would have previously inspired Rose to run a brush through her hair and apply fresh lipstick. But it wasn't as if Dalton hadn't already seen her at her worst. She wasn't thinking only about their argument, but that maybe she had, in a sense, used him. And for that, she was deeply sorry. Ashamed.

A soft knock sounded on the door, and she ran to it, flinging it open and throwing her arms around the only man aside from John that she'd ever even thought she could love.

"I'm sorry," she said into the warmth between his neck and shoulder. "You have to know I never deliberately set out to hurt you. I just wanted my pain to go away."

"Did it?" he asked, backing her up to step inside and shut the door.

"Yes…" She wanted to stand there in the cocoon of his arms forever, but for what she had to say, even that felt somehow wrong. So she retreated to a kitchen bar stool, needing, for some unfathomable reason, to say what she had to say alone. "For a few incredible moments when we were together, the pain was gone. All I could think about was the possibility of an amazing future—with you. But then I was hit with the guilt."

Setting his keys on the counter, Dalton climbed onto the stool beside hers. "You vowed till death do you part. What don't you get about the fact that you've parted?"

She sighed. "This is exhausting. We just keep talking in circles. Believe me, I know everything you're saying is true, but it's one thing to say it and another to believe it, live it. Your situation with your dad really isn't all that different. If you leave the bank, you stand to potentially lose his love and respect. I think he'd eventually get over it, but in the short term it'd be hard."

"You're right," he said with a grim-faced nod.

"So if we're both right, why do we feel wrong?"

Sharply exhaling, he held out his hand to her and she took it. "Sleep with me," he said. "No funny business. Just sleep. Blessed, mind-numbing sleep."

Holding on to his hand for all she was worth, she led him to her bed.

"Hi, Mr. Dalton!" Anna said, jumping on Rose's bed.

Dalton groaned, rubbing his right hand over his eyes. He'd meant to be up and out of the loft before the little girl woke, but clearly that plan had fallen through. Time for plan B—whatever that was.

"Mommy, I didn't know you were having a sleep-over. Let's have pancakes!"

Sunlight streamed through the loft's soaring windows. Rose looked soft, beautiful and tousled and Anna had scampered off to the kitchen, where she was now banging pots and pans. Completeness swelled Dalton's chest. The feeling that here, with these two girls, maybe he'd finally found home.

"You're still here." Rose cast him a luminous smile.

"Where else would I be?" he answered with a wink.

"Mommy? Where's the pancake stuff?"

"How'd you sleep?" he asked, brushing strands of hair from her eyes.

"I slept all night, if that tells you anything."

"Mmm…" he said with a manly swell of pride. "Looks like these arms of mine are good for something."

"Mom!"

Rose grinned. "Duty calls."

"Let me," he said. "You stay here and lounge."

"Sure?"

Kissing the tip of her nose, he said, "Absolutely."

Rose chose to take a shower instead of lingering in bed. Then she helped Anna get ready for school while Dalton prepared their breakfast feast.

At first, she'd been terrified of what Anna might think or say about Dalton having accidentally spent the night. She'd been ashamed, worried what the neighbors might imagine. Moreover, what John might have thought. But neither she nor Dalton had planned on falling into such a deep sleep. It just happened. Sort of like the way, without either of them knowing it, they'd started to take on the feel of a family whenever the three of them were together.

As much as she still feared the idea, she'd also begun liking it, trying it on for size.

Soon, the scents of coffee brewing, bacon frying and pancakes browning in a cast-iron skillet filled the loft. Dalton had set the table, cleaned a few dozen strawberries he'd unearthed in the fridge, then called the girls to the table.

"*Dese* are *woot*," Anna said, mouth loaded with pancakes.

"Don't talk with your mouth full, sweetie."

"I know," the girl said after swallowing. "But, Mom, they're really good."

"What can I say?" Dalton preened. "When you've got it, you've got it. I'm a natural when it comes to the kitchen."

"A natural-born disaster," Rose teased, eyeing the splattered mess.

"I'll clean up after myself."

"You'd better," she said with a wink. "My biweekly manicure is this morning. No way am I canceling because a cooking diva like you trashed my kitchen."

"I'll stay home and clean, Mommy."

"I'll bet you would," Dalton said, ruffling the girl's silky hair, which felt even softer than her mom's.

"Hey, I'm a good dish washer."

"Yes, you are," Rose said, "but you're even better at spelling, and I don't want you to miss your new word list."

Carrying her plate to the sink, Anna made a face.

Rose whispered, "Sure you want to have kids?"

"More so than ever," he said, giving the child a wistful glance as she shoved crayons, a Barbie and a Matchbox car into her My Little Pony backpack. "Anna, what grade are you in?"

"First. But I'm smart enough to be in fifth."

"I don't doubt that for a minute," he said, snatching his and Rose's plates. "Do you drive Anna to school?"

"We're in a car pool. This is her friend Abbey's week, but I should get her downstairs to wait."

"Hurry back," he said, craving a kiss but not wanting to be overly affectionate in front of Anna.

"Baby, you ready to go?"

"Uh-huh. Bye, Mr. Dalton! Have a happy day!"

"You, too," he said, answering her wave.

With the little dynamo out of the loft, the space suddenly felt enormous. By the time Dalton finished the dishes, Rose was back, gifting him with a bright smile and proper good-morning kiss.

"That's more like it," he said, settling his hands low on her hips. "Some men need coffee in the morning, but I'm thinking all I need is you."

"Likewise," she said with another kiss.

"Hey, I'm sorry I was still here when Anna got up. I'd planned on setting my cell's alarm to wake me in an hour, but we fell asleep before I got the chance."

"It's okay," she said, adding soap to the dishwasher, then starting the load. "At least I think it is. I have to admit, when she first bounded in, I was worried about how she'd take finding you here, but she really didn't seem all that surprised. Guess that's because she likes you."

"I suppose. Still, I wonder if she'll have questions for you this afternoon when she gets home."

"That would be understandable, seeing how I have questions myself."

He took her hand, eased his fingers between hers. "Got anything I can help figure out?"

His cell rang.

"Damn. I'm found." On his way to fish the phone from his jacket pocket, he said, "Whatever you were about to say, hold that thought. Hello?"

"Son," his father bellowed into his ear. "I don't know where you are, but you'd better get your rear down to the bank ASAP."

Click.

Grimacing, Rose said, "The man's loud."

"You think?" Flipping the cell shut, Dalton sighed. "You can't imagine how tired I am of this. His need for control."

When he lowered onto a bar stool, she slipped her arm around his shoulders. "Do you think his testiness has to do with his heart condition? His fear that he's got to get everything done in a hurry, just in case he doesn't live to see another day?"

Dalton laughed. "With any other man, I'd agree with

you and cut him some slack. Trouble is, William Macy Montgomery popped out of his mother's womb barking instead of crying, and he's been doing it ever since."

"I guess that means you're leaving?"

"Eventually. First, I thought I might have a second cup of coffee, then read the paper. After that, how about we take a leisurely stroll through the park? It's supposed to be another gorgeous day."

"All of that sounds amazing, but, Dalton, don't you think you'd better do as he asked? I mean, there's no sense in getting him any more worked up. You'd never forgive yourself if something happened to him."

"Relax," he said, drawing her in for a kiss. "The man will outlast us all. He's too damn stubborn to do anything but."

"HEY, MISS ROSE. Good to see you," Frank said when she helped herself to her favorite booth at the deli. "I don't know where you learned to perform miracles, but you must've gotten an A+."

"Oh?" she answered, sipping the raspberry tea he'd been kind enough to remember she always ordered. "What did I do that's so miraculous?" Other than have the best night's sleep she'd had since before her husband's death.

"Mona and Alice. They're back together. Alice called me last night to say she's already planning the costumes for your little tykes' dance routine."

"That's great," she said. "Any idea what look she's going with?"

The waitress brought a bowl of homemade chips.

Frank slid into the booth's empty seat, helping himself to a handful of the yummy treats. "According to my wife—she works down at Hobby Mart—Alice has cooked up some kind of Carmen Miranda theme with loud orange dresses and fruit bowls on the girls' heads."

"S-sounds nice," Rose said, barely avoiding choking on her latest chip. Fruit bowls? Wow. Oh well, at least she wasn't having to make them.

Famous last words.

That night, after she and Dalton had tucked in Anna, they sat at the kitchen counter, assembling elaborate hats.

"Tell me again how we managed to get roped into this?" Dalton asked.

"Making an amazingly long story short, Mona got stung by a bee and Alice had to take her to the emergency room. If we don't get the hats done, Alice won't have time to sew the dresses, seeing how the pageant's only a week away."

"Right," he said, scratching his head. "Why didn't I think of that?"

After hot-gluing a plastic banana to a plastic pineapple, she gave him an elbow nudge.

"Ouch," he complained. "You made me get hot glue on my thumb."

"Poor baby," she said, drawing the wounded appendage to her mouth for a medicinal suckle.

"You keep that up," he said, "and this hat assembly line is being tossed out the window."

"Oh?" she asked, eyebrows raised. "And what, pray tell, might we be doing instead?"

He whispered all sorts of naughty suggestions into her ear, but then straightened. "Sorry. I forgot that we weren't going to do any of that anymore until after you give the all clear."

"It's okay," she said. And oddly enough, for the moment, it was. Maybe Dalton had been right, and time really was all she needed to thoroughly heal.

"Sure?" He stopped her in the middle of gluing grapes to what she guessed was a pomegranate.

"Positive." He looked relieved, but not as relieved as she felt that the two of them were able to have such an open and frank discussion without Dalton getting upset or her bursting into tears. "How did things go with your father this morning?"

"Got an hour?"

"Sweetie…" She eyed the mound of plastic fruit lining the counter. "From the looks of this mess, I've got no less than five. Tell me every detail."

"Hi, Mr. Dalton!" Anna said, jumping on the foot of the bed. Rose was missing, but the scent of frying sausage, coffee and something cheesy gave him a clue as to what she'd been doing. "Sleepovers are fun, huh?"

Dalton shot the girl a tight grin. He'd only meant to shut his eyes for a second. He was still in his suit pants and now-funky instead of crisply starched white shirt. As he was starting to do more and more often, he'd drifted off on top of the covers, but was now toasty beneath a colorful quilt. He for sure hadn't meant to indulge in another heavenly night with Rose. It wasn't good for any of them—especially Anna, who was no doubt confused.

Albeit, she was still jumping. "I don't have school today because of parent-teacher conferences. That means we'll have all morning to play."

"That's cool," he said. "Wish I got days off of work for stuff like that."

"Maybe you should start going to school with me," Anna said, showing no signs of stopping her jumping anytime soon. It was making him dizzy just watching all that early-morning action. But she also made him happy.

What must it be like to wake each day with joy instead of dread? He had to make it a priority to find out.

"Anna!" Rose admonished, emerging from the bathroom with hair wet and red velour jogging suit clinging to her curves. "How many times have I told you to stop jumping on the beds?"

"Lots," Anna said, snatching a few more quick leaps before scrambling to the floor. "But it's just so fun. Mr. Dalton thinks so, too."

"Hey," he said with a wide smile, arms behind his head, "don't bring me into this. Your mom looks pretty mad."

"She'll be okay. Back before Daddy died, we all used to jump on the beds."

"Anna!"

"What? It's the truth."

Ignoring her child in much the same way Dalton ignored the underlying tension, Rose hustled off to check whatever smelled so great in the oven.

Anna hightailed it to her room.

Dalton shut himself in the bathroom to splash cold water on his face, frowning when his watch told him it was already past nine. Damn, he'd had no business sleeping so late.

In the kitchen, the coast clear from snooping-kid eyes, he snagged Rose around her waist and stole a quick kiss. "Good morning. I'm starting to like waking up beside you. Only trouble is, this morning, you weren't there."

"Sorry," she said. "Now that I've slept through the night again, thanks to you, I feel energized. Like I'm ready to take on the world. Only instead of doing quite that much, I figured I'd make you a nice breakfast. You know, something to jump-start your day."

He groaned. "My day was supposed to start about three hours ago, so it looks like Anna's the only one who'll be jumping around here."

"I should've woken you. But you looked so at peace."

"Yes, you should have gotten my lazy butt out of bed, but thanks for not doing it. I've gotta say, the extra shut-eye felt great. Oh—thanks for covering me, too."

"You're welcome."

"FRANKLY, ALICE, I'm not sure whether to turn him over my knee or ground him. He just doesn't seem to have the passion he should, considering the responsibility he's about to be handed."

"Gee, Dad," Dalton said, strolling into his father and Alice's impromptu break-room meeting, "correct me if I'm wrong, but it seems to me that I already do pretty much everything around here except occupy your fancy corner office."

"Dalton," Alice admonished, "don't you dare speak to your father like that."

"Alice," Dalton said, standing his ground, "would you mind giving Dad and me a little privacy?"

"William?" She looked to his dad for permission. As did everyone else in the building whenever the great man was around.

"Go on," he said. "I'll be fine."

Ha!

"All right, then. Stop by my office when you're done, and I'll get you that printout you wanted to go over."

"Will do. Thanks." Alice shut the door behind her.

While his father brewed, Dalton calmly fixed himself a cup of coffee.

"Son, I don't have all day," he finally barked while Dalton took his time adding one sugar packet, then two. "Kindly get on with your explanation of what's gotten into you. You haven't been acting at all yourself."

Maybe that was because ever since meeting Rose, he hadn't been feeling himself. "Trust me, Dad, I'm better than I've been in years."

"You'd sure never know it by your performance

around here. Alice said you've been coming in late and leaving early. She suspects it's because of that tango instructor. What do you have to say on the matter?"

"I *know* it's because of the tango instructor, and you were the one who insisted I grab a few more lessons—remember? So I'd be sure not to shame the family with my lack of dancing prowess? I hardly think you're in a position to complain."

"Are you and this woman serious?" his father asked, snagging a cookie from the center of the break room's table.

"Put that down. You know you're not allowed to eat it. And what if Rose and I *are* serious? Would you object?"

Ever defiant, ever master of his domain, his dad didn't just take a bite of the cookie, but ate the whole damn thing, then proceeded to down another. "You know your mother has her heart set on you marrying Miranda Browning. Now, she's a nice girl. She belongs to our club. Our world. *Yours.*"

"I know Mom means well, but she wouldn't be the one spending the rest of her life with some nice girl from the club."

"So you're saying it is serious? This fling you're having with a dance teacher? For heaven's sake, Dalton, did your divorce teach you nothing? Plus, she has a daughter. Did you know that?"

Clenching and unclenching his fists, Dalton said, "It's taking everything in me not to slug you."

"Slug me? What did I do? Other than shower you

with love and everything money could buy? Then top all of that off by giving you your own bank?"

Shaking his head in disbelief, Dalton left the room before he did something they would both regret.

FIFTEEN MINUTES LATER, he arrived at the dance academy. The parking lot was full, save for a spot at the very back.

In the lobby a group of leotard-clad, white-haired women clamored around the reception desk.

He politely hovered behind them until he and Rose and the throbbing Latin bass from studio three were all that remained in the room.

"What's wrong?" she asked, stepping out from behind the desk to smooth his forehead. "You look awful—not that you aren't still handsome as ever, just that—"

"I know," he said, taking her wrists, drawing her hands down. "I have an odd favor to ask."

"Sure. Anything."

"If it's not too much trouble, could I use your loft for the rest of the afternoon? I want to work on my sculpture. It somehow…" He shrugged. "It just seems like the right thing to do."

"Of course you can, *mi novio*. Stay as long as you like or need."

"Thank you," he said, pressing a kiss to her cheek, then leaving her to take the stairs two at a time.

Slanted shafts of sunlight lent the loft a churchlike feel. He opened the fridge, planning to grab a bottled water, but spotting an open wine bottle, he chose that instead. If he was going down, might as well do it right.

Taking the protective sheet from his sculpture, he surveyed his work. He drank deeply, and for a long time just stared at his creation, at the infinite nuances left to be explored.

Rose's face, gentle with sleep. Her throat, arched in passion. Breasts, swollen with desire. Her hands… When she held him, he was capable of conquering the world on his own terms—not his father's.

Eyes open, he set the wine on a side table and breathed. Drawing the room's warm air slowly in through his nose, and out through his mouth, willing his pulse to slow.

Everything would be okay.

He wasn't sure how, but everything *would* be okay.

Approaching the sculpture stand, he glanced down, surprised to find his hands trembling. Funny, how different the piece looked with Rose in the room, urging him forward. Alone, he was lost, confused. He hadn't realized how much Rose had come to mean.

Tentatively, he fingered the damp clay. It was cool to the touch, smelled of earth and rain and somehow Rose, herself. Her goodness. Her deep well of emotions and endless depth of spirit. Thinking of her, only her, he put aside his nerves and embraced the work.

With just his fingers and the rudimentary tools Rose had bought him, he molded and shaped the clay until slowly, Rose was there, not in the physical sense, but in the spiritual. His mind's eye caught her hair streaming behind her in a danced leap. Her arms flung high in a joyful abandon he'd never before known but would certainly like to try.

His work took on a fever pitch.

For the first time since sculpting in college, he experienced the wonder of being so engrossed in a project that he forgot the time and place. All that mattered was the flow of creativity sparking from his fingertips to the clay. All that mattered was Rose, and the fact that she'd made this pleasure possible.

He hardly knew her, yet in a sense, he owed her everything. She wasn't in any way like his ex-wife. Rose was just her sweet, beautiful self.

Stepping away, hands and back sore, he realized the piece was done. The room had grown dark, and it only just now occurred to him that Rose wasn't there. All afternoon, he'd lovingly kneaded her curves, stroked her lips, breasts and thighs. She'd been as real to him as the air he breathed, but now the illusion was shattered.

He'd stepped out of his dreamworld and into a cold, empty loft, and a heart that didn't feel much better.

Chapter Eleven

"Why'd we have to go out to eat, Mommy?"

Rose eased the lock into the back door, opening it slowly to first check if Dalton was still working inside.

A cursory glance showed her the coast was clear.

"Mr. Dalton was working, honey."

"On what?"

"His sculpture," she said, flicking on the overhead lights, then hefting the two grocery sacks she'd carried to the kitchen counter.

"Whoa. Look, Mommy. It's you."

Rose finished putting the milk in the fridge, then spun to look where Anna was pointing. She was blown away by the incredible likeness of herself.

Hands to her mouth, tears welling in her eyes, Rose moved closer to the sculpture. Dalton didn't just have talent, he was phenomenally gifted. For him to spend his days locked in an office when he had this kind of gift to share with the world was a crime.

"Did Mr. Dalton really make this? Or did he just buy it while we were at the store?"

"H-he really made it," Rose stammered. "Pretty amazing, huh?"

"Yeah. Can I take it to show-and-tell?"

"I don't think so, sweetie. It might be kind of hard to fit in the car."

"Oh. Can I have some of the Oreos we bought?"

"Sure."

"You want some?"

"No, thank you."

While her bottomless pit of a child chased off in search of her latest snack, Rose backed onto the sofa's arm, trying to remember the last time she'd faced such quality artwork. New York? London? The lines and proportions were flawless. Even more incredible was that Dalton had made the creation in two days. For his father to deny—squash even—this level of god-given talent was shameful.

In his heart, Rose believed, Dalton knew that. But how would she ever convince him to act upon that knowledge?

"MISS SHREVEPORT, while I appreciate the fact that you've been amply blessed," Alice said in a stern tone, eyeing the girl's heaving, turquoise-sequined bosom, "please keep in mind that this is a family-oriented event."

"Yes, ma'am," the blonde said in a slow drawl as she practiced her dance moves onstage at Hot Pepper's municipal auditorium.

"Now, where were we?" Alice asked Rose. "Oh—the staging for your production numbers. Flanking the stage will be three giant chili peppers representing the past, present and future of our city. At the stage's center, you'll have an approximately twenty-by-fifteen-foot area for use at your discretion for choreography. Will that be sufficient?"

"Sounds perfect," Rose said. "Are the costumes done?"

"All but one. Stephie Jenkins's mom fibbed about her daughter's waist size. She'll be over tonight to get fitted for alterations."

"Thank you."

"You're welcome. Thank you for agreeing to the added performances. I think it will not only add flavor to a normally dull portion of the pageant, but should also drum up new interest in your dance studio."

Miss Houma bolted across the stage, clutching a fire baton and three hula hoops.

"That would be wonderful. When Miss Gertrude retired, many of her students left with her. I'd be happy for the new business."

"Interesting you should mention that," Alice said. "I had a talk with William Montgomery this morning, and he seems to feel Dalton has taken his dance lessons too seriously. They've begun to jeopardize his job performance, and this is a crucial time in the bank's growth."

"That's ludicrous," Rose said. "There's no such thing as being too engrossed in dance."

"Yes, well, in Dalton's case, I beg to differ. Not to get into your affairs, but Dalton can't afford any distractions."

"Is that what you think I am?" Rose asked.

"Now, I didn't in any way mean that to be offensive, just that you're relatively new to Hot Pepper, and as such, it's understandable that you wouldn't be familiar with our ways."

"Your ways? Does this have something to do with the fact that I'm of Latin descent?"

"No. Lord, no. I meant *our ways* as in small-town business. We work very hard here. We have friend-ships, but it's helpful if relationships overlap. You know, in a meaningful manner that could be beneficial to both parties."

"Kind of a 'you scratch my back, I'll scratch yours' thing?"

"Exactly," Alice said with a brilliant smile. "Here's the thing. We all like you. You're lovely, kind-natured and talented. But, sugar, Dalton was born to bank, and you were born to dance. Judging by the time he's been spending away from his office lately, the two vocations don't mix."

"SHE SAID WHAT?" Dalton fumed from his perch beside Rose on her sofa. He was glad Anna had long since fallen asleep.

"Had I known you'd get this upset, I never would have told you." Finger-combing his hair from his forehead, she said, "Laugh it off. That's what I did. The very notion is archaic. It smacks of a time when there were arranged marriages between landowners to increase holdings."

"I'm going to see my father right now. He's got to be stopped." He pushed to his feet.

She stood, urging him back down. "Nothing can ever be solved by fighting. Understand, this is the only way he knows to do battle. What you must do is take the high road. Show him that you're more than capable of having both a happy home life and successful business life."

"Is that what we have?" he asked, stroking her cheek. "A happy home life?"

"I know I'm happier when you're here. So is Anna." She fixed him with a misty-eyed stare. "Are you?"

"What?"

"Happier when you're here?"

"Of course," he said, lacing his fingers with hers. As usual, he ignored the sliver of doubt still lingering in his gut. They weren't talking forever, but about the here and now. And here—now—he was happy. "But I'm not remotely happy at the office."

"Then what are you going to do?"

"What can I do? If I quit, I'll give my dad a potentially life-ending heart attack. If I don't quit, I'll probably keel over myself by age forty. If I give you up, my friends and family will apparently be overjoyed. I, on the other hand, have started craving you like an addiction."

Raising her feet onto the sofa, Rose snuggled against him, resting her head on his lap. "An addiction, huh? I have a penchant for funnel cake, whenever I can get it."

She winked.

He tightened his jaw. "I'm serious."

"I can see that. But why?"

"Why?" He half laughed. "Because you've got a beautiful little girl who deserves all of you, and I'm a mess. You don't have time for a guy like me."

"Shouldn't I be the judge of that?"

"WHY DO I GET the feeling you're avoiding me?" Rose asked Dalton backstage at the pageant's dress rehearsal.

"I couldn't tell you," Dalton said, adjusting the red satin tie Alice and Mona had made him wear with his black tux and red satin shirt.

"Lookin' good," Frank said to Dalton, hustling by with a platter of hoagies.

Dalton rolled his eyes. "I look like a cross between Cupid and an undertaker."

"You do not," Rose said, hoping to smooth things between them. Why, she wasn't sure. By his own admission, he wasn't the man for her. But if that was true, why, with every breath of her being, did she suspect he just might be?

Ignoring her worries, along with the noise level created by twenty chattering contestants and their mothers, Rose raised her hand to Dalton's forehead, on the verge of caressing him like she'd done dozens of times before. But he ducked away from her, consulting the schedule he held in his hand.

"Looks like it's about our turn."

"Uh-huh," she said, close to tears. Dalton was an amazing man. Anna already loved him. Rose felt as if she could so easily love him, if only she could let go of her fears. She was trying. Why couldn't Dalton do the same? "Dalton?"

"What, Rose?" The look he cast her wasn't cold or cruel, but impersonal. As if he'd washed his hands of her.

"Nothing, I—"

"Rose!" Mona shouted from the wings. "You and your little ones are on!"

The stage lights came up. Fifteen girls in fire-orange dresses with fruit on their heads giggled out from the wings. Dancing with her protégées, Rose fought past the lump in her throat, forcing a brilliant smile. She battled the urge to see if Dalton stood in the wings watching.

All too soon, Rose was alone onstage as the lighting and music took a sultry turn.

Dalton stepped from stage right to join her.

Ever the gentleman and professional, he offered her his hand. As much as his eyes denied his attraction, his body couldn't lie. The heat between them was palpable, and as the lights dimmed and music rose, they were spot washed in light, and danced beautifully.

Even though tonight was only a practice run, Dalton's moves were flawless. He danced as if he'd been born to it. But while technically his performance was perfect, there was something missing.

The soul. Spirit.

When the music ended, Dalton made a hasty escape

to the opposite side of the stage. Before she was able to ask if they could talk, he'd vanished into a crowd of leaping human fruit bowls, giggling beauty queens and anxious stage moms.

"Mommy?"

"Hey, sweetie," she said. "You did great. You, too," she said to Anna's friend Becca. "I'm proud of you both."

The music she'd selected for Dalton's dance with the outgoing Miss Hot Pepper boomed, turning Rose's attention back to the stage. To Dalton. To the undeniable fact she wanted to be the woman in his arms instead of the beauty queen he currently held. While his performance was flawless, it lacked passion. This observation warmed her. Told her that whether Dalton mentally acknowledged their being right for each other or not, his body—more importantly his spirit—already knew.

"Mom-mee?" Anna's voice had raised to a whine. "I came over here to ask if I can spend the night with Becca. Can I?"

"I'll have to talk with her mom to make sure it's okay."

Ten minutes later, the sleepover was arranged, and Rose had kissed her daughter good-night.

Heading for the stage-crew lounge, she searched for the snack table, hoping Frank would be nearby. Sure enough, he was.

"Hey there, Teach. You and Dalton really tore up the dance floor."

"Thanks," she said.

"Hoagie?" He offered her one of the two sandwiches he held.

"No, thanks. You could help me out with something, though."

"Name it."

She took a potato chip from the table and a plastic cup filled with Coke. "I, um, need to talk to Dalton, and he's not answering his cell." Considering she hadn't even tried his cell, Rose supposed she should at least cross her fingers over the lie. But seeing how badly she wanted to see Dalton face-to-face, she hoped her fib was justified. "You wouldn't happen to have his street address, would you?"

"I couldn't tell you the mailing address, but could probably give you a fair set of directions and a description of his house."

"That'll do." She fished a pen and notepad from her purse.

Nose scrunched, he asked, "Haven't you been to his place before?"

A nervous laugh escaped her. "It's funny, but we usually hang at my loft. You know, since Dalton's always there anyway for his lessons."

"Sure. Makes sense."

He took a bite of his sandwich, then told her the way.

ROSE SQUINTED through the drizzle on what had turned into an especially black night, and hoped she'd found the right house. She pulled her Jetta into the driveway of the oak-ringed, two-story southern colonial that looked big enough for a family of eight.

The lights were out save for one in a rear side window. She looked for signs of Dalton's presence, but if his SUV was there, he'd parked it in the garage.

Figuring she owed it to herself to at least see if he lived in the mini-mansion, she turned off the engine and trudged on a winding brick sidewalk.

With a deep breath, she stepped up to the front porch.

One more breath gave her the courage to ring the doorbell.

When no one answered, she rang again.

Shoulders hunched against the damp chill, frustration tight in her chest, she'd turned for her car when the door opened.

Wearing jeans and nothing else, Dalton stood back, gesturing for her to come inside.

Avoiding the sight of his smooth, muscled chest, she instead focused on the immense formal dining room off to her right. The *empty* formal dining room. The entry hall was more of a two-story gallery. A staircase gracefully arched to a balcony that would be amazing for a bride intent on making a grand entrance. The white marble floor inlaid with black marble diamonds was both elegant and serene, the blank walls—eerie. As best she could tell, the whole place was vacant of furniture, and life.

Arms crossed to ward off a shiver caused not by the weather but the massive void, Rose said, "I, um, like what you've done with the place."

Dalton sighed and shoved his hands in his pockets. "Where's Anna?"

"She has a sleepover with Becca."

He nodded. "She did well tonight."

"I thought so, too. In fact, everyone did an amazing job. I wasn't expecting it to be such a large production."

"Why are you here?" he asked.

"I'm not completely sure." Edging past him, she boldly left the entry for what she guessed was the living room. In front of a lifeless fireplace was a card table and folding chair.

Beyond that, a two-story family room, also with a fireplace, that looked over a chef's dream of a kitchen. Also…bare.

"Do much entertaining?" she asked, carrying a half-dead ivy to the sink for a shot of water.

"I try to be here as little as possible. The place has never been my style."

"Why'd you buy it?"

"I had to live somewhere. This house is as good as any."

"I'm hungry," she said, opening the fridge. No great surprise, the looming space echoed like the Grand Canyon. "Yum. Ketchup, mustard and olives. Oh—and pickles."

"There's Chinese takeout in there somewhere. And apples and oranges in the crisper. And look," he said, pointing to the side door, "three eggs. Now, when are you going to tell me why you're here?"

"I'm here because I want to be with you. You're my friend, and I can't stand this wall between us."

"I'm sorry. I don't mean for there to be one."

"Yet here it is." She grabbed the pickles, unscrewing the lid to fish one out. "Now, what are we going to do about it?"

"What do you want to do?"

"For starters, stop talking in circles. The other night, you accused me of not having time for you, but it seems to me, the way you shut me out tonight, that the statement should be the other way around."

Washing his face with his hands, he groaned. "Again, I'm sorry. There's just a lot going on. I care about you, Rose. I care about Anna. But with so much on my plate, I feel like I should be focused on that. Not worrying about you 24/7."

"Did I ever ask you to?" She took a bite of her pickle, then winced before spitting it into the disposal side of the sink. "Yech. Are you trying to kill me?"

"Sure. I didn't even know you were coming, but just in case, I stocked my fridge with poison-laced kosher dills."

At that, she couldn't help but smile.

And then he was smiling.

That led to full-on laughing from both, until somehow, Rose had melded herself against Dalton's strength. Hugging him for all she was worth, she hadn't realized until that moment how much she needed him.

How much she loved him.

Yes, *loved* him.

Only not in the way she'd loved John, but in a special way reserved all for Dalton. Despite that realization though, the question she couldn't keep from asking centered around one simple thing—was love enough?

Enough to overcome the past?

Enough to sit by and watch Dalton make a mess of his future?

He wouldn't be happy at the bank, yet being the noble soul he was, he also wouldn't be happy destroying his father by up and announcing he wanted nothing more to do with his current job. Lately, she'd begun to wonder if there might be even more on his plate than he'd told her about. Some deeper reason behind his refusal to see that what they shared was a rare and amazing gift. One he seemed ever more willing to throw away.

Chapter Twelve

"Mommy?" Anna said during the ride home from Becca's late Saturday morning. The Hot Pepper Festival was in full swing, and traffic was insane. "What's *shacking up?*"

Rose was so startled by the question she nearly rear-ended the white Taurus in front of them. "What did you just say?"

"When me and Becca were cooking Pop-Tarts, Becca's mom was talking on the phone in their dining room and me and Becca heard her say you and Mr. Dalton are 'practically shacking up.'"

"Nothing," Rose said, gripping the steering wheel till her knuckles shone white. "That means absolutely nothing you need to know about."

"If it doesn't mean anything, how come Becca's mom said it?"

Rose counted to ten in her head, willing the red light they'd been stopped at for what felt like the past year to change.

Last night's rain was still falling.

She flicked her windshield wipers to high.

She felt sorry for the festival's vendors—craftspeople, food sellers, game and ride operators and the like—suffering through the rain. Yet it certainly hadn't seemed to affect the number of folks in town for the three-day event. The city park had to be swamped with both puddles and people.

"Mommy? Why'd she say it?"

Sighing, wishing her child had forgotten the matter, Rose said, "Sometimes, when two grown-ups really like each other, they practice being married. Do you know what slang is?"

Anna shook her head.

Swell.

"Slang is just a different way of wording things. Like instead of saying we're going to have lunch, some people might say they're grabbing grub or breaking bread."

"Oh."

"When Becca's mom said Mr. Dalton and I were—you know." Lord, she couldn't even bring herself to repeat it. "She just meant—" in a hateful, gossipy way "—we enjoy spending time with each other."

"Are you?" Anna asked once they'd finally turned off the main road and onto a quieter side street.

"Are we what?"

"Practicing getting married? And if you did get married, would that mean Mr. Dalton would be, like, my second dad?"

Never had Rose been so grateful to pull into the alley behind their loft home.

"I think he'd be a fun dad. He makes really good pancakes. And when he reads me stories, he does funny noises. He snorts the best of anyone I know."

Turning off the engine, Rose unbuckled her seat belt, then angled to face her daughter. "Sweetie, there's a lot more to someone being a good dad than that."

"I know. He has to know how to change fire-alarm batteries, too. We learned that on our field trip to the fire station."

"Yes, that's also important, but moms do that job, as well."

"I know. Can we go inside? Becca loaned me a new ball gown I wanna try on my Ballerina Barbie."

"Sure," Rose said, kissing the top of the girl's head.

With Anna in her room, Rose made a pot of coffee, hoping to ward off the afternoon's chill. But what she couldn't escape was the hurt stemming from being the center of ugly gossip. Up until her encounter with Alice, and now this, Rose had only seen the nice side of small-town life. But then in all fairness, the dance troupe she and John had been with was always a hotbed of rumors.

It wasn't even the fact that her and Dalton's relationship was being discussed that hurt, but that she doubted in her heart whether there even was a relationship. Really, though they'd made love, there was no commitment on either of their parts.

Never had the saying "so close, but yet so far" been more appropriate.

And if there were a commitment?

If after tonight's performance, Dalton fished a gorgeous ring from his pocket, then asked her to marry him, what then? Would she do it? Would she be anywhere near ready to open herself to loving again?

What about Anna? Would she also put her daughter's heart at risk over a man she hardly knew?

"THIS IS SWEET of you," Rose said to Dalton as he held open the door for her and Anna to the best steak place in town. They were eating early because they all had to be at the pageant by six-thirty.

"Seeing how you're paying," he said with a wink, "I figure getting the door is the least I can do."

"You're so funny," she said with a poke to his steely abs.

"Hey, it was worth a try."

Soon, they were seated in an intimate corner booth Rose suspected was usually reserved for couples, but since Anna was engrossed in coloring her kids' menu, she and Dalton might as well have been on a date.

After a waitress brought iced tea for Rose and Dalton, and orange pop for Anna, Rose discreetly mentioned what her daughter had overheard Becca's mom saying.

Shaking his head, Dalton said, "I went to high school with Kari. She was always a vicious gossip, as was her mom. Not that this will make you feel any better, but just so you'll know, this attitude is targeted more toward me than you. Kari's best friend, Misty, and I had a fling a few years back. I'm thinking Misty had her heart set on marriage. I was just looking for someone to take to the bank's Christmas party. When I see her around, she still looks at me like I'm the devil." Laughing, he sipped his tea. "Women."

"Hey," Rose complained. "Not all women have nothing but weddings on their minds."

"True," he said with a sweet kiss to her cheek. "And in other not-so-fun news…I spoke to my father today."

"Oh?" She reached for a sugar packet, dumping it into her tea.

"He and Mom will be there tonight. He said they were hoping to meet you after our performance."

"Considering the whole town seems to be against us becoming a couple, that'll be something to look forward to."

"No one feels like that," he said.

"Alice does. She's the one who flat out told me I'm not good enough for you, seeing how I don't have a pedigreed background."

"Stop," he said, taking her hand, smoothing the top with his thumb.

"Eeeuw," Anna said, glancing up from coloring. "Mr. Dalton, why are you holding Mommy's hand? Are you two going to kiss?"

"Would you think it was yucky if we did?" Dalton asked.

She took a moment to consider. "Well, if you gave her one of those really long movie kisses, that would be gross. But I suppose just a nice kiss would be all right."

"Thank you for your permission," he said.

"Well?"

"Well, what?" he asked. Rose wanted to crawl under the table from embarrassment.

"Aren't you going to kiss her?"

Dalton wanted to kiss Rose. But seeing how it was a gross movie-type kiss he'd had in mind, he figured he'd better wait until Anna went to bed.

"Know what?" he ended up saying.

The little girl shook her head.

"Instead of kissing your mommy, I think I'll just kiss you instead." He scooted the few inches between them and kissed the top of her head.

"Eeuw," Anna said with a huge smile, pretending to wipe off his germs. "You're gonna get it." Now she was the one sliding, and she got revenge by planting a big wet one on his left cheek.

"Eeeeeuuuw," he said right back, being sure to make a properly repulsed face even though her actions had him secretly touched. "You're disgusting."

"No, you are," she teased.

"I heard you eat bugs," he said.

Not to be outdone, she retorted, "I heard you eat boogers."

"That's enough," Rose said, apparently declaring herself the grown-up of the bunch. "You two stop right now, or I'm putting you both in time-out." While her words sounded menacing, her eyes smiled.

"She started it," Dalton said, pointing at Anna.

"No, you did." Anna's face brightened with a grin.

Luckily, the argument was settled by the arrival of two T-bones with all the trimmings, and Anna's corn dog. They settled into their meal while conversation and laughter flowed. The contrast between this trio and Dalton's own family trio was startling. In the home where he'd spent the first eighteen years of his life, he didn't feel as at ease as he did right now in a crowded steak house.

"You all right?" Rose asked.

"Never been better," he said, grinning.

"Then why are you frowning again?" She touched his cheek.

With Anna again engrossed in coloring, Dalton felt free to say, "I was just thinking how right this feels. The three of us."

"How is that something to frown about?"

"It's not," he said, telling her what she wanted to hear.

"If y'all are half as nervous as I am about who's going to win the crown," Mona said with a titter, wincing under the spotlight's glare, "then you'll be happy to know we have more of this fine, Hot Pepper–style entertainment to keep you on the edge of your seats till that crown's placed on our lucky winner's head."

Rose's talented little girls had already bobbed their

fruit bowls for the cheering crowd, so it was now time for Rose and Dalton's performance.

Standing in the wings alongside her, he leaned in to whisper, "Can you say microphone hog?"

"Stop," Rose said. "She's not used to being in front of a crowd."

"If someone had a rope, we could lasso her and get her away from the crowd."

"You're terrible."

"I try," he said with a devilish wink.

"Without further ado," Mona rambled on, "I would like to introduce you to two of Hot Pepper's brightest dancing stars. It's a long-standing tradition here at the pageant to showcase our incoming chamber of commerce president in a tango, and this year, as a special treat, Mr. Dalton Montgomery will not only perform with the outgoing queen, but also with Rose Vasquez, a world-renowned professional dancer." Mona stepped back to wave them onstage.

Though Rose had performed all over the globe, she had never suffered from a worse case of nerves.

Then Dalton smiled and took her hand, giving her fingers a gentle squeeze. He mouthed, "You look beautiful."

The next four minutes passed in a blur of whispered touches and fervent glances. The passion between them was rekindled. As was the attraction that had first driven her into Dalton's arms. As the music swelled, so did her heart. He was a wonderful man. He was good for her.

Good for Anna. Just because she'd opened her heart to let him in didn't mean she had to block John out. Her memories of him, of nights like this, sharing the stage together, would always be with her. Only now, she'd make new memories.

There, in Dalton's arms, Rose felt as if she'd finally come home. Finishing to thunderous applause, hand in hand they took a bow.

At that moment, Rose vanquished all thoughts of what Becca's mom or Alice might think of their pairing. As all of these cheering people could plainly see, the two of them belonged together.

Would their relationship one day evolve into something more? Maybe even marriage? She couldn't say. All she really knew was that for the first time in a long time, she felt happy. Complete. And for the moment, that was enough.

Surrendering her man to the outgoing queen, Rose wistfully smiled at the sight of him expertly maneuvering the girl across the stage. He might temporarily have another woman in his arms, but she was the woman he'd go home with.

"OUR NEW MISS HOT PEPPER is…" Mona's hands shook while reading the news from the judging form. "Miss Shreveport, Chelsea Prioux! Congratulations, Chelsea!"

The town's orchestra launched into their version of the Miss America theme song.

"Here she is…" Alice sang in a falsetto, "Miss Hot *Pepppp-errrr…*"

Amidst cheers and confetti and balloons, Dalton took Rose's hand, tugging her close. Into her ear, he whispered, "That should be you up there. Clearly, you're most deserving of the crown."

"Clearly, you're delusional. Did you see how the girl looked in her swimsuit?"

"You forget, I've seen how you look in your birthday suit, and it's a pretty amazing sight. Definitely worthy of a crown."

"You need crowning," she teased.

"On a serious note," he said, putting his arm around her waist and leading her to a backstage area where there weren't so many crying or giggling girls, "I thought our dances rocked. Thank you. My father and fellow pageant-committee members will be proud."

"You're the one who should be proud, Dalton. When I think of how far you've come in such a short time…" Her eyes welled. "I believe you're one of my best students."

"Students?" he teased, while a prop guy whistled by, giant hot pepper in his arms. "I'm not sure I'm comfortable being referred to as a student."

"Truthfully…" she said, inching him into a forgotten corner, then kissing him with hungry abandon, "I suppose we have moved our relationship in a more intimate direction."

"Then maybe we should get a babysitter for Anna tonight. Unless…" Hand beneath her chin, he tipped her face back, peering into her soft brown eyes. "Where does John fit into all of this?"

Swallowing hard, she shook her head. "Onstage, something in me changed. No one will ever be as strong a tango partner as John. Dancing was his life. But you, Dalton Montgomery, have skills all your own that flow so nicely with mine. Dancing with you tonight, I felt like we were a couple. With your help, I've finally realized that love is a precious gift—not to be feared, but cherished. I can't let fears of what *might be* ruin the magic of what already is. I love you."

Holding her for all he was worth, Dalton breathed in her musky exotic scent, and reveled in the feel of her molded against him.

"Let's go home," she said, the words warm against his throat.

"Do I get to stay the night?"

"Duh." Her grin dazzled. "It's pretty much become your home, too." Rose pulled out her cell phone and made arrangements to drop Anna off at the sitter's.

Arm in arm, Anna giggling ten paces behind with her friends, they left the stage and wound through the crowd. It felt good to be a unit, the three of them against the storm. Not that the crowd was particularly unruly, but losing queen candidates and their families weren't exactly the most chipper of folks.

They'd just made it to the auditorium doors when Dalton groaned.

"What's wrong?" Rose asked.

"Trouble to our right. Want to run, hide or face it head-on?"

She swatted his forearm, then, with a warm smile, greeted his parents and the trio they had with them. "Mr. and Mrs. Montgomery. I'm Rose—Dalton's dancing instructor. It's so nice to finally meet you."

"Likewise, dear," Dalton's mom said, warmly grasping Rose's hand. "Dalton speaks of you often."

"In glowing terms, I hope."

"Absolutely," said Miranda. She held out her hand, introducing herself and her parents, as well. "The performances were wonderful. You two should be proud."

"I know I am," Rose said. "Dalton?"

Chuckling, he tightened his hold on Rose. "I'm just glad it's over."

"Miranda is quite an accomplished ballerina," his mother said.

"Mmm… My husband and I used to hold season tickets to the Texas Ballet Theater," said Rose.

"You were lucky," Miranda's mother said. The woman, like her daughter, was tall, pale and thin. She was undeniably beautiful and unfailingly polite. Mrs. Browning had spent a lifetime becoming the perfect corporate wife. She'd groomed her daughter for the same. She should be the perfect woman for him.

Only one problem—Rose was the woman his pulse raced for.

"We're headed for a late dinner," Dalton's father said.

"Son, how about joining us." It wasn't so much a question as a command.

"Thanks, but Rose and I already have plans."

"She's welcome, too. Rose—that is," Miranda's mother interjected. "I'll call the club and ask Bernard to add one to our reservation."

"Thank you," Rose said.

"Yes, thank you," Dalton added, "but really, we have plans."

"Son…" His father's stony glare said what his words didn't: Do it, or else. Only, Dalton was no longer a heartbroken kid straight out of a disastrous marriage. He wasn't hungry for a job or desperate to find his place in the world. At the moment, the only world for him was Rose's. "Your mother and I would very much like for you to join us."

"I appreciate that, Dad. But what *I'd* very much like is to spend the evening with Rose—alone."

Chapter Thirteen

"Man, that was exhilarating."

Rose glanced across the front seat of Dalton's SUV. After they'd dropped Anna off Dalton had really started to loosen up. He tapped his fingers in time to an Aerosmith classic, and in the glare of lights from oncoming cars, appeared breathtakingly handsome and strong. "What was exhilarating?"

After stopping for a light, he clasped her hand, bringing it to his lips for a kiss. "Telling my parents, no."

"Not something you do often, I take it?"

"Not nearly enough."

"Miranda's lovely."

"She's not half as pretty as you." Releasing her hand, he accelerated through the light, down Cincinnati with its historic, redbrick storefronts and white lights in the trees.

"Think you can charm your way out of it, huh?" She rubbed his shoulder.

"Out of what?"

"It's kind of obvious your parents and Miranda's would like nothing better than for the two of you to be together."

"And…" He turned left, then sharply veered right, narrowly avoiding a pair of revelers who looked a bit tipsy from the festival's beer garden and square dance.

"And so that left me feeling like a third wheel back there."

"You're being silly."

"Am I, Dalton? The whole time we've been together, I've sensed you holding a part of yourself back."

"What part?" He turned onto the side street leading into the alley behind her loft.

"I don't know." She crossed her arms, hesitant to break the light banter with a serious subject, yet feeling as if it needed to be done. "I just thought you might have a secret."

He laughed. "A secret? Like a hidden tail? Or maybe a penchant for eating bananas during full moons?"

"Stop," she said, gently squeezing his thigh.

Pulling up behind the loft, he turned off the lights and killed the engine.

"I'm being serious."

"Like I'm not?" He winked. "I've gotta say it's going to be one helluva relief to get that tail out in the open. I've been having awful cramps."

Shaking her head, grinning despite herself, Rose unfastened her seat belt. Clearly, he was avoiding her probing question, but that was okay. By choosing her over both Miranda and his parents, he'd told her that he took her and their relationship seriously. But had he grown to care for her as much as she and Anna cared for him?

THEIR LOVEMAKING that night was tender and slow. And when morning dawned with sunshine drenching the bed, Rose took it as a sign that as that weekend's dismal weather had passed, so had her life's storm.

Easing from beneath the covers while Dalton was still lightly snoring, she pressed a kiss to his smooth forehead. Then she had a leisurely bubble bath in the oversize soaking tub.

Eyes closed in contentment, she prayed Dalton would wake feeling this good. She prayed for him to have a sense of grace and clarity in regard to his life's direction. Of course, he shouldn't abruptly quit the bank without some other plan in place, but as miserable as he'd been, it was high time he focus on life's beauty for a change.

Contentedly wriggling her toes, she shook her head. Since when had she become such a Pollyanna?

"This a private party? Or can anyone join in?"

Grinning up at Dalton, she scooted back, making room. "By all means, please, climb in."

He did.

She added more hot water and bubbles and soon, bathtime had been transformed into fun time with kissing and splashing and laughing till her sides hurt.

He'd shifted to the rear of the tub, pulling her atop him. Eyes closed, kissing him, she abandoned herself to his spell.

"Thank you," he softly said. "You've awakened creative parts of me I'd feared forever lost. For that, I'm not sure how to repay you."

"Nonsense." Tracing his lips, she said, "I'm the one who should be thanking you."

After another kiss, he said, "How about if we count to three, then give mutual thanks?"

"Sounds like an excellent plan."

"Okay… One, two—"

A muted electronic sound pierced the loft's morning hush.

"What was that?" Rose asked.

Dalton groaned. "My cell."

It finally stopped.

"Do you need to answer?"

"Definitely not. Where were we?"

"Counting."

"Ah, yes. One—"

The phone rang again.

"This is why I've never wanted a cell. Seems like they always ring at the worst possible time."

"Ignore it," he said, hand at the back of her head, urging her lips to his. "No doubt someone at the bank misplaced a file, or can't figure out how to unjam the copy machine."

The phone's chirpy electronic tone stopped, but started right back up.

"You'd better get it," Rose said. "Sounds like whoever it is wants you pretty bad."

When it stopped, Dalton said, "See? Whoever it was, they wisely went away."

"Go," Rose said, easing off of him so he could get out of the tub.

With a whoosh of water, he pushed himself up, snagging a red towel from the rack, wrapping it around his waist. "I'm sorry about this."

"It's okay." She loved the sight of him. Muscular shoulders and back, radiating strength. The incongruous picture he made wearing only a towel while taking what was obviously an important call brought on a giggle. Then a defeated edge to his posture erased her urge to laugh.

Shoulders sagging, he said, "Of course. I understand. I'll be there as soon as possible."

Be where? she longed to ask, but waited until he'd set down his phone.

"Dalton?" She rose from the tub, wrapping herself in a towel before going to him. Hands pressed against his chest, she dared ask, "What's wrong?"

A muscle ticking in his jaw, he wouldn't meet her gaze. "I have to go. My father had another heart attack."

DALTON DROVE to the hospital more recklessly than he should've, but he figured what the hell did it matter if he got a ticket? Worse yet, rammed himself into a telephone pole? He couldn't physically hurt more than he already did.

Rose had begged him to let her come along to the

hospital, but he gave her the excuse that since his father was in intensive care, no one but family was allowed to see him.

Rose had told him she wouldn't be at the hospital to see his father, but to support him. He'd still refused because secretly, he didn't want her witnessing the end of their beautiful dream. In the harsh light of day, that's what the two of them were. With his dad so ill, he could no more leave the bank than he could change his eyes from blue to green.

One call, and all his hard-won resolve had vanished. He'd been plunged headfirst back into the role of prodigal son.

He finished the trip without incident, only to find that the nurses wouldn't let him in to see his dad.

The head nurse led him to a windowless, beige waiting room, which was dark except for a pool of light from a corner lamp. Stale coffee and desperation scented the air.

A man with a small girl—maybe age two or three— on his lap slumped in a recliner at the far end of the room. An elderly gentleman pretended to be reading a battered copy of *Reader's Digest,* but his eyes kept darting to the door.

Beside a dark TV sat Dalton's mother, looking ten years older than her age. When she saw him, she smiled, and he was filled with guilt for ever having put his own needs ahead of hers.

"How are you?" he asked. When she rose, he gave

her a hug. She seemed frail and smelled faintly of arthritis cream. When had she grown old?

"I'm fine," she said. "We were having breakfast at the club when it happened. Your dad was in the midst of a heated debate over whether or not we should do like some of those bigger banks, and stay open till all hours of the night, when it happened. Alice was here, but I sent her home. I know she'll need to be in the office early in the morning, and I figured there was no sense in her sitting around when they won't even let us inside." When she shivered, Dalton removed his lightweight jacket, slipping it over her shoulders. Sinking back into her chair, she said, "Your father's doctor sees no reason why he shouldn't recover, but I have to tell you, it does my heart good knowing he won't have to worry about the bank. I know he doesn't always show it, but he's been so impressed by your work, Dalton. He's very proud of you."

Lead settling between his shoulders, Dalton backed into the chair beside her.

His mom patted his knee. "You've always been such an asset to him—to us both. We love you."

"I love you, too," he said, thinking of Rose, wishing he'd told her he loved her before leaving. Only just now did he realize that fact. He loved her. But because of that love, he owed it to her to not get her mired in his messy life.

A nurse entered the waiting room, prompting all present, save for the sleeping girl, to look up. "Montgomery family?"

"That would be us," his mother said.

"Mr. Montgomery is awake and asking to see his son."

Not sure he was ready to see his dad, Dalton said to his hollow-eyed mom, "You go. I know how much you must want to be with him."

She shook her head. "Right before his doctor wheeled him into surgery, your father asked for you. He's worried about you, Dalton."

"How can he be worried about me? I'm not the one who just had emergency heart surgery."

"Sir?" the nurse prompted, lightly touching his shoulder.

"Right," he said. "Let's go."

Out in the hall, they faced a set of double metal doors. The nurse pressed a square button on the wall that opened the doors with a soft *whoosh*. Inside was a harsh, white space that looked straight from a sci-fi movie. Machines hummed and beeped. The air was cold, thick with the scents of cleaning fluids and antiseptic.

The nurse stopped outside a room labeled #7. She opened a sliding-glass door, then gestured for Dalton to step through. He wasn't entirely sure he wanted to.

The ghostly pale man lying in the bed wasn't the daunting figure Dalton had always thought him to be. His father was no longer intimidating, but in need of his son's help and support. There was no way Dalton could think of leaving the family business now. No matter how much he loved Rose, he couldn't walk out on his dad when he needed him most.

Sure, over the years, his father could have given him more independence, more latitude in choosing his own career, but all of that was water under the bridge.

Dalton's future was clear.

"Son. You came." Though his father's raspy voice sounded barely human, Dalton acted as if the man whose voice had always boomed thunder hadn't changed a bit.

"Where else would I be?" Dalton asked. They'd never been a demonstrative family, but he took the older man's hand in his. When his father squeezed tightly, Dalton knew he'd done the right thing.

"I need to talk to you," his dad said. "Set a few things straight."

"It's okay. I know I haven't been keeping the most regular hours lately, but—"

"No—" his father clutched Dalton's hand harder "—this has nothing to do with business."

Then what? The man knew nothing but business.

"I—I want to talk about regrets."

"Okay…" Dalton glanced beyond the sliding-glass door. Where was the nurse? Had she given his father too much pain medication?

"Ever since my first heart attack, I couldn't help but wonder at the path I'd chosen for my life. Back when I went into the family business, I wanted to be a banker, just like my pop." Dalton winced when his dad emitted a throaty chuckle. He didn't sound good. "There hasn't been a single day I've spent at the bank that I haven't thanked my lucky stars for the life I've—we've—been given. That said, folks talk. I'm hearing you're not as happy at the bank as I've been." He coughed again. "I—I guess what I'm asking in a roundabout way, son, is if you have any regrets."

Where did Dalton start? If he told his father the truth, would he die right here on the spot? "Regrets. Dad? I'm not sure what you mean."

"I mean, are you happy? Does running the most respected and lucrative, family-owned financial institution in our corner of the world make you truly, bone-deep happy?"

How Dalton longed to answer truthfully, but what good would truth be if the pain of that truth caused his dad to suffer another attack? In the end, Dalton took a deep breath and said, "Sure, I'm happy. Why wouldn't I be?"

BY ELEVEN MONDAY MORNING, Dalton was buried so deep in files, a snow shovel would be needed to clear them. Still, he doggedly kept at it, as the alternative—breaking up with Rose—seemed far worse than being up to his neck in work.

"Mr. Montgomery?" Joan said through the intercom. "Ms. Vasquez is here to see you."

"Send her in." Wearily standing, he washed his hands over his unshaven cheeks. What would he say to her? Was now the time to do the deed in breaking things off? Or should he wait until they were in a kinder, gentler setting?

Like the sun easing out from behind clouds, she glided into his office. At first, she was smiling, but that was soon enough replaced by a frown. "My God," she said, cupping her hands to his cheeks. "*Mi novio,* you look horrible." Sweetheart. She'd called him her sweetheart. Last time she'd called him by the Spanish phrase, Dalton had looked up the meaning. Hands now around his waist, she hugged him tight. "I'm so sorry. How is your dad? Is he going to be all right? I waited for you to call, figuring you must be with family. But when you never did, I had to come see you for myself."

"How did you know I was here?"

"I stopped by the hospital first. Your mom told me where to find you."

"You saw Mom?"

"I'd kind of have to see her to talk to her, wouldn't I?" When he didn't crack a smile, she elbowed him.

"That was a joke."

"Sorry," he said, releasing her to rake his fingers through his hair. "Guess I'm not much in the mood for clowning around."

"Understandable," she said, helping herself to one of his guest chairs. "So? How is he? What happened? Your mom looked pretty rough, so I didn't want to bother her."

Back in his chair, Dalton said, "Dad had an emergency bypass. But his doctor thinks he'll be fine just as long as he lays off cream sauce, bourbon and cigars."

"Rats." Rose made a face. "That pretty much rules out the finer things in life, huh?" Reaching across the desk to take his hand, she said, "You should be home sleeping. Even better, you should be at my home sleeping."

The mere suggestion of closing his eyes in Rose's big, comfy bed had him yawning. "As good as that sounds, I have a lot to finish up here."

"Anything I can do to help?" she asked, leaving her chair to perch on his lap. She wore a pale lavender sundress trimmed in white lace that made her dark skin look especially edible. Never had there been a more gorgeous woman. Never had he been more resolute in what he needed to do. She and Anna deserved a man who'd live for them. His father had told him that as soon as he left the hospital, he'd announce his retirement, officially handing the reins to him. If Dalton was this miserable to be around now, Lord only knew what kind of bear he'd become when the bank was solely his.

"I wish you could help, but…"

"Will you at least let me fix dinner for you tonight?"

He'd like nothing better, but dare he risk spending more time in her arms? On the flip side, her home would probably be the most comforting place for her to be when he ended things. He would let her down easy. Explain why she and Anna deserved so much better than him.

"Dalton? Dinner?"

"That, um, sounds great, but I have to go to the hospital."

"I know, but surely you're not spending the night, are you?"

"No, but—"

"All right, then. Anna and I will expect you around eight. Think that'll give you time for a nice long visit with your dad, or should we make it later? Why don't you invite your mom? I'd love to talk with her under more pleasant circumstances, and she could no doubt use a change of scenery."

"Rose, I—"

"I know, you're busy." Draping her arm atop his shoulders, she leaned in close for a kiss. It wasn't a passionate kiss or a casual kiss, but somewhere in between. In the realm of dear friends or that of a comfortably married couple. It was a kiss that spoke of love and respect, caring and trust—none of which he felt worthy of receiving. She got to her feet and kissed him again, then said, "Don't overdo it, okay?"

Without waiting for his reply, she left the room, marooning him with only a lingering trace of her perfume and a rising sense of despair.

Chapter Fourteen

That night, after visiting with his mom and dad and a few aunts and uncles he hadn't seen since Christmas, then stopping by a grocery store for flowers and a liquor store for wine, Dalton was running about fifteen minutes behind schedule.

"I've been worried about you," Rose said when he let himself in the loft's back door. She stood at the stove, face flushed from steam rising from a cast-iron pot. "What took so—"

"Mr. Dalton!" Anna raced from her room, tossing her arms around him. "I missed you. Mommy said your dad's sick. Is he going to be okay?"

"Sure, sweetie," he said, kissing the top of her head. Lord, but he'd miss this child. But if there was one thing he'd learned from his father, it was that he didn't want to raise a child in anything less than a one hundred percent happy home.

"Me and my bunny are watching *Shrek*. Wanna come

watch with us?" She took his hand, dragging him toward the loft's TV area.

"Thank you for asking, but I need to talk to your mom. Will you pay close attention so you can tell me what happens?"

"Okay." After gifting him with another hug, she scampered off. His throat constricted painfully. How the hell was he supposed to do this? He wasn't just breaking up with one girl he loved, but two.

"In case you haven't noticed," Rose said, buttering an open loaf of French bread, "she adores you. Her mom does, too."

Dalton's heart shattered.

"You're late. What took you so long?"

"These." He handed her the gifts. "Am I forgiven?"

"Always." Checking out the label on the pricey merlot, she said, "You have good taste. Plus, the wine happens to go with our main course."

He sniffed the savory air. "Spaghetti?"

Rose grinned when Dalton's face lit up at the prospect of indulging in his favorite meal. Thank goodness spaghetti was indeed on the menu. She didn't want to let him down. Not even on something as simple as Monday-night dinner.

"How'd you guess?" From a shelf next to the sink, she took a cobalt-blue vase.

He pointed to his nose. "I've always had a knack for sniffing out my favorite foods."

"Really? In all the time we've been together, I've never noticed that about you."

He shrugged.

"How's your dad?" she wondered aloud, filling the vase with water.

"Better. But he seems different."

"How?"

"Hard to explain." He sat on one of the counter bar stools. "He's always been the strictly business type. You know, all numbers and no emotion. Yet the last couple times we've talked, he's asked some pretty strange stuff."

"Like what?"

"Questions about my goals. If I'm happy."

"That's fantastic," she said, setting the fragrant bouquet of mini-irises, daisies and daffodils on the counter. Resting her elbows on the cool tile edging, she asked, "Did you tell him how you feel? You know, about pursuing a career other than working at the bank?"

"Not exactly."

"Ah," she said, plucking a wilted daisy petal. "Which must be why you seem on edge."

"I'm fine," he insisted.

"If you're so fine, how did you manage to misplace an entire dinner guest?"

"Huh?" Nose scrunched, he asked, "What're you talking about?"

Rose counted to ten in her head. He probably had a perfectly good explanation for not having brought his mother. "I asked you to invite your mom. I even scrubbed the bathroom in her honor, so why isn't she here, Dalton?"

"She just couldn't make it, all right?"

"Did you even ask her? Or are you for some reason ashamed of your relationship with me?" That last question caught in her throat, and she hastily looked away.

What was wrong with her, carrying on like this? Why did it even matter whether or not Dalton wanted her to get to know his mom and dad?

Dammit, it mattered because Dalton mattered. Rose had admitted loving him. Her daughter loved him. For better or worse, by whatever twist of fate, their lives were already irrevocably intertwined.

"Rose, relax," he said, getting up from his stool and wrapping his arms around her. "There's no deep, dark motive. I just forgot. What with work and then the hospital, I—"

"It's okay," she said. She didn't want to hear his explanations, because if she truly loved him, she wouldn't need them. She had to learn to trust. "I'm the one who should be sorry. You have enough to deal with without me piling my insecurities on top of your already full load."

"No, really. This was nothing more than me being overwhelmed with work. Mom and Dad will love you."

"You think?"

"I *know*. You're smart, talented, beautiful. What's not to like?"

"Suck-up."

"Yes, ma'am." He winked.

Together, they finished meal preparations, then talked over the delicious food and merlot while Anna performed magic tricks with her napkin.

By the time the candles burned low, Rose had learned all sorts of new and tantalizing facts about her guy. He'd won the school spelling bee in sixth grade, harbored a secret penchant for Cap'n Crunch cereal, and did pretty amazing magic himself by adding or subtracting four-digit figures in his head.

Once Anna had declared them boring, and the grown-ups finished off the wine, Dalton admitted how much he wanted to be a father one day. If Rose hadn't already been over the moon in love with him, that last bit of information would have done her in.

"Do you want a boy or a girl?" she asked, running the tip of her toe up his inseam.

"One of each."

"Nice if you can pull it off, but how do you plan on guaranteeing success?"

"Simple, by picking the perfect mom."

Assuming by the misty smile Dalton shot her way that she was the woman he had in mind for the job, Rose's heart beat faster. Pushing back her chair, she reached for his plate.

"Let me," he said, hand over hers. "You cooked. I'll clean."

"You'll get no argument from me."

While he tackled the mess, she sat on a bar stool, finishing her wine. He made fast work of loading the dishwasher, then scrubbing the pots and pans.

He washed down the counters.

Scoured the sink.

"You're awfully industrious—and quiet." Hopping up, she set her glass on the tile in front of her. Then she rounded the counter and slid her hands up his back, massaging his shoulders. "Talk about tight. When's the last time you took a vacation?"

He reached over her shoulder, finishing off her wine. "I thought one day with you was the equivalent of a week at a spa."

"That's what everyone says, but evidently, you're immune to my restorative powers." Working her thumbs deeper into his muscles, she asked, "Worried about your dad?"

"Mmm-hmm." Dalton closed his eyes and stopped polishing the soap dispenser to focus on her. Her musky smell, her gentle yet strong touch. Her way of making him feel like the luckiest man alive to have ever been held in her arms. He'd planned to let her down easy, but how, when their bond grew steadily stronger? "I wish I didn't have to go back to the hospital."

"Then don't. It's late. Odds are, your dad won't even be awake."

"I have to go back because it's my duty."

"Dalton, you've got to learn to make time for yourself. How can you help your dad if you let yourself get run-down from stress? You need to learn that nobody has to do anything they truly don't want to do."

If only that were the case. "You don't get it," he said, searching for something else to clean. "My dad just suffered his second heart attack. He's worked his whole life to make our bank a respected organization. His father before him did the same. I can't let his dream *and* him die. I can't. *Won't.*"

"Yes, but—" she stopped rubbing his shoulders to turn him to face her "—don't you see? That's your father's dream. What's yours?"

He sighed and bowed his head while drying his hands on a dishrag. "Before meeting you, it had been so long since I'd thought of anything but the daily grind, I'd all but forgotten how to dream."

"All right, then," she said, taking him by the hand to lead him to the sofa. "Here's what we have to do…"

"Whoa," he said, halting her progress. "I have to finish cleaning in the kitchen. I always finish what I start."

"Great." Releasing his hand, she finished the short trip to sit down. "Remind me to give you a Brownie point at the end of our session. Come here," she urged, patting the cushion beside her.

"Really, I need to—"

"*Grrrr,* you're a stubborn man. Please," she begged. "Humor me for just a few minutes, then you can not only organize the contents of my cabinets, but bleach the grout."

"Okay," he said, plopping onto the end of the sofa farthest from her. Why couldn't he just break up with her? Why did he keep drawing out the pain? "What do you want me to do?"

"Lay your head on my lap."

"With Anna fifty feet away?"

"I've watched and heard this movie thirty times. We've got about fifteen minutes until the end. Now, please, lay your head on my lap."

Because he was still too cowardly to accomplish what he'd come for, he did as she asked. "Okay, I'm down. Now what?"

Fingers stroking his temples, she said, "I want you to breathe."

"I am."

"No, really breathe—from here." She pressed his abdomen, and just the heat of her touch seeping through his thin polo shirt woke parts of his body he willed back to sleep.

"Excuse me," he said, "but I think you're starting something you may not be able to finish."

"Stay still, and keep your mind out of the gutter."

Holding out his hands in surrender, he said, "Okay, I give up. You win."

"That's better. Now, take another deep breath."

"I already did."

"Do it again."

He complied.

Rubbing her fingertips up and down his temples, she said, "Think back as far as you can and tell me what your first dream was."

"Easy. To kiss Jodi Foster. She was hot back in those Disney movies." A mischievous wink shot her way.

Rose chuckled and rolled her eyes. "As big a fan as I am of Ms. Foster's work, that wasn't the reply I was looking for. Try again."

"I don't know what kind of dream you mean."

"A work dream. What did you want to be when you grew up?"

"An astronaut, first, then Jodi's boyfriend, second."

"I'm ignoring that second part, but the first one was good. What else did you want to be?"

"A pastry chef. Ours was really good, and he let me eat his mistakes."

"Your family had their own pastry chef?" She couldn't even imagine such wealth, but far from envying Dalton's privileged upbringing, she felt sorry for him. Seeing the pent-up man all that money had created made her eyes sting for the lost little boy.

"Hey, cut me some slack. He only came in three days a week. After all, how much pastry can one family eat?"

"Good point. Anything else you wanted to be?"

"A gardener. Andrew made really great topiary animals. His grouping of lions in my parent's formal garden is one of the best I've ever seen—and I've traveled a lot."

"Wonderful. We're finally getting somewhere. Anything else?"

"A chauffeur. Charles spent half his time driving cool cars, and the other half caring for them. Could there be any better job than getting paid to play with cars?"

"Sounds good to me." She grinned, sweeping a fallen lock of hair from his forehead. "That it?"

"Yep. That about covers childhood aspirations. Of course, in college, I went through that artistic phase, but then doesn't everybody?"

"No. I mean, I guess my dancing would be considered an art, but my brothers all went to trade schools. They love working with their hands. Which, if you look back over the fields you just told me about, pretty much shows that you might enjoy working with your hands, as well."

"Especially whenever I'm around you."

"I'm serious," she said, gesturing to where his sculpture stood before the darkened window. "Look how beautiful your work is. You have a God-given talent that it's a sin to waste on cold, hard facts and numbers."

Splayed hands against his chest, she said, "Your heart beats so warm, *mi amor*… Why do a job that's so cold?"

He struggled beneath her. "Let me up."

"Not yet." She held him down, close, just a few seconds more. "First, tell me you're completely happy with your current line of work."

"I'm happy," he said, voice as flat as a warm can of pop. "There, I said it. Are *you* happy?"

"No. This isn't just about words. I want you to do something special with your life. To wake in the mornings and say to yourself, 'I'm thrilled to be alive.'"

He shot her a thunderous look, then struggled to his feet. This time, she let him go. Maybe she'd overstepped her bounds, but what she'd told him had needed to be said.

"I've got to go," he said. "Thanks for the great meal."

"Don't leave mad. I'm sorry if I offended you. I was only trying to make you see what I have from the start."

"What's that?"

She stood, too, and with her hands pressed to his chest, she quietly said, "I see inside you, Dalton Montgomery. You have the raw material to be a fantastic artist... If only you'd open yourself up and let him outside to play."

Dalton sighed. "That would be nice, but my father's lying in a hospital bed, inches from death's door. What kind of man would I be if I abandoned the one thing in his life he cares most about in order to search for my artist's soul? Doesn't that sound selfish to you?"

"No, it doesn't. And I'll tell you something else. Judging by the talk your dad tried having with you, I don't think the subject of your happiness would sound selfish to him, either."

"I have to go," Dalton said, clutching his chest. "Say bye to Anna."

"What's wrong? You're not having pains in your heart, are you?"

"No. Just indigestion."

"You get it a lot."

"So?"

"You should see a doctor."

"You should mind your own business."

Tears welled in her eyes at his incredible insensitivity. "I thought you were my business."

"Lord, Rose, what am I doing?" He pulled her close, crushing her with his hug. "I'm sorry. I never meant to hurt you."

"It's okay. I'm strong."

"But you shouldn't have to be. You deserve a man who treats you like the amazing woman you are. You deserve so much better than me."

"But it's you I want."

"Then maybe you need to reassess *your* dreams."

Chapter Fifteen

Long after Dalton left, Rose couldn't get his harsh words from her mind. The nerve of him. Telling her to reassess her dreams. Her dreams of what? Being a mom? A dancer? Sharing her love of dance with anyone who cared enough to learn? She'd already achieved those dreams. That only left dreams for her personal life, and since, at the moment, all her future aspirations centered around Dalton, that made his cryptic statement even harder to bear.

Had he been warning her that he wasn't as perfect for her as he seemed? Worse, did he carry a secret in his heart? A secret he was either too proud or too cowardly to share?

Mind swirling with pain, Rose got Anna settled for the night, then put herself to bed. But when her head touched the pillow, all that happened was a lot of tossing and turning.

When they'd last made love, she'd been certain she and Dalton would be together forever. He'd been so tender. His touch whispery soft, yet at the same time, powerfully erotic. A man who put so much effort into lovemaking could never conceive of hurting her, could he?

She drew the covers close. Alternately hating and loving the way they still smelled of him. She'd have stormed out of bed to wash them, but a simple sheet washing would do nothing to cleanse him from her soul.

Long into the night, she watched silver moonlight cast a longer shadow from her sculpture. Why hadn't he started another one? What was holding him back? Whatever debt he felt he owed his father? Or her?

"JOAN!" Dalton barked into the intercom to his secretary, sounding suspiciously like his father. "Have you seen the Rogers file?"

"Nope. Want me to help look?"

"No. Thanks, though." Casting a frantic glance about his desk, he gritted his teeth. His stomach started churning.

He was on the verge of asking Joan to come help him after all when she magically appeared at his desk, much needed file in hand.

"You're a saint," he said. "Where was it?"

"Carrie in accounting found it on the break-room table." She wiped at a smudge on the manila folder's corner. "It has ranch dressing on it, but other than that, seems none the worse for wear." She stepped back to appraise him. "You, on the other hand…look awful."

"Thanks."

"Rough night?"

"The worst."

"I just spoke with your mother, and since your father's doing well, and expected to be released this afternoon, I'm guessing this has something to do with a certain gorgeous brunette who's been a frequent visitor?"

He pressed his lips tight.

"Want to talk about it?"

"No."

"Everyone has tiffs, Dalton. Plus, as a benefit to fighting, afterward you get to make up."

"I said I don't want to talk about it."

"Okay, okay. I'll leave you to sulk in peace. Oh—and sorry about messing with you about your file. I had it all along. Alice put me up to it."

"Figures," he said, his voice not quite as rough as it had been. Alice was his right-hand man—or rather, woman. She'd been working for the bank a decade before he'd even been born. Childish pranks were her fountain of youth.

Joan waved, then returned to her desk.

She hadn't been gone five minutes when Dalton was back on the intercom. "Did you really just say my father's being released today? Isn't that too soon?" *And why the hell was I the last to know?*

"Miracles of modern medicine. Oh—and before I forget, your mother asked me to tell you not to make plans for Saturday night."

"Why not?"

"She and your father have booked the club to throw

a party. He's going to announce his retirement, then name you his successor. Sounds fun, huh?"

Dalton clutched his chest. "Have you seen my antacid?"

IN THE DANCE ACADEMY'S lobby, the damn fountain gurgling happily as ever, Dalton took a deep breath, then slowly exhaled. He didn't want to do this, but if he truly loved Rose and Anna, it was the right thing—only thing—to do.

Latin bass pulsed through the studio walls, bringing to mind the many hot nights he and Rose had shared. If only things had been different. If only his dad hadn't been sick. If only his parents had seen fit to have a bigger family, with lots of heirs.

Too bad for him, *if onlys* wouldn't get him anywhere. With his dad's big party planned for Saturday night, the sooner Dalton made a clean break from the life he so desperately wanted, the sooner he could return to the life he'd been given.

Right on schedule, Rose released her senior-citizen samba class. He lingered in the hallway's shadows, watching her easy smile and the way all of her students seemed to love her—including him.

When the crowd had finally thinned, he cleared his throat. "Rose?"

She jumped. "Dalton. You scared me. How long have you been back there?"

"Not long. I wanted to let you finish before interrupting your day."

"*Mi novio,* you're not interrupting, but enhancing." She kissed him, then locked the front door. "I've got an hour before my next class. Let's head upstairs and I'll feed you."

"That sounds great," he said, pulse raging, acid roiling up his throat, "but I don't have time."

"Oh…okay. But if you don't have time to be here, why did you come?"

"My dad's being released from the hospital today."

"That's wonderful. I'm so happy for you—him, too."

Dalton shifted his weight from one leg to the other. "Yeah, well, here's the deal. Saturday night, my folks are hosting a party at the club."

"How fun. I hope there's going to be dancing." She snapped her fingers and wriggled her hips.

Meanwhile, he cleared his throat, praying for strength for himself, and understanding from Rose. "I couldn't say about the dancing. Dad's announcing his retirement. Naming me his successor."

"How do you feel about that?"

"Resigned."

"Honey, you have to say something. Get out now, while you can."

"That's just it," he said. "Seeing my father in that hospital bed made me more determined than ever to do just that. Get out now. Only not from the bank, but from whatever lunacy led me to forget everything I am in being with you."

Rose needed air.

This couldn't be happening.

"Dalton?" She went to him, put her hands on his shoulders, but he wrenched free of her hold. "Honey, we can work through this together. Who says you can't work at the bank and have a satisfying home life? It doesn't have to be all or nothing."

He snorted. "That's where you're wrong. I'm miserable at that job. Do you honestly think that's ever going to change? Say we stay together, get married, have a couple kids of our own, what happens when my misery causes me to being grumpy with you or the kids? What happens if I do like so many other guys in my family's sainted social circle and turn to booze or other women to drown my sorrows?"

"Oh, Dalton," she said, forcing him to look at her, smoothing his brow. "You would never do any of that. You're too good, too pure."

"You may think that now, but there are no guarantees, Rose."

"I know you're hurting, Dalton, but why do you have to hurt me, too? Why can't you lean on me to help you through this? Why do you insist on being Mr. Tough Guy? Handling everything alone?"

"Because," he railed, gripping her forearms. "That's the way it has to be. I love you, Rose, but I love my family, too. If I leave the bank and it fails and my mother ends up penniless and on the street? How the hell would I live through that, knowing her pain was a direct result of my selfishness?"

"*Her* pain? What about mine, Dalton? For one second, would you please forget your parents and look at me. Really look at me. I love you. Anna loves you. The three of us, we've become a family. Your parents are capable of taking care of themselves. It's time for you to focus on *you*, on us."

"I can't," he said, holding her tight. "I'm sorry, but my sense of duty is too strong."

"Your sense of duty?" she asked, stroking his hair. "Or your fear?"

He remained silent.

"I'm right, aren't I?" she probed. "You have been harboring a secret, haven't you?"

He wouldn't meet her gaze.

"Dalton? Honey, I love you. You can tell me anything. I promise, I—"

"Look, I was married, okay?"

"W-what?" It wasn't that the notion was so outrageous, but how could he have kept something like a previous marriage from her?

"Carly and I met in college. One of those love-at-first-sight kind of things that never should have happened. Bottom line, things didn't work out. She soon saw I wasn't who she'd thought I was—an artsy free spirit, ready to roam the world on a whim. She took all our savings, donated it to the Save the Whales fund, then ran off to Bolivia with some guy in the Peace Corps."

"Oh, Dalton... You must've been devastated."

"You might say that."

"But, sweetie, what does any of that have to do with me? Why did you feel you couldn't tell me? Carly sounds like the one who lost out on an amazing man."

He snorted.

"You disagree?"

Sharply looking away, he said, "We're getting off the subject. The point I'm trying not too successfully to make is that in Carly, I chose poorly. She was from a world I didn't belong to." Gripping her shoulders, he gave Rose a light shake. "Don't you see? I don't belong in your world, either. I don't know where I belong. But until I figure it out, I owe it to you and Anna to steer clear. You both deserve more than my wishy-washy brand of companionship."

"Companionship? You really think that's all we share?"

"I don't know," he said, pacing. "That's the point. How am I ever supposed to know if what we share is the real deal? Or just another shortsighted mistake?"

"If you even have to ask," she said softly, "you're absolutely right. What we've shared has been a mistake. A big one."

"YOU LOOK LIKE you've been rode hard and put up wet."

Dalton glanced up—a long way, considering he was lying on the ground with his shoes and socks off, wriggling his toes in the city park's grass.

Alice stood over him, jogging in place. "Well? What's wrong with you?"

"Not that it's any of your business, but I'm sick, all right?"

"Lovesick."

"Leave me alone." He closed his eyes, annoyed by the intrusion.

Not only did Alice not leave, but she plopped her Lycra-covered butt down beside him. "I had a talk with your lady friend."

"Yeah," he said without opening his eyes. "She told me about it. How you practically flat out told her she wasn't good enough for me, and that I needed to move on to someone my mother would approve of."

"I said nothing of the sort. I was testing your Rose. Seeing how bad she wants to be with you. Since the day you were born, you've been a pocketful of trouble, Dalton Montgomery. Too handsome and talented for your own good. I don't know how many teachers told your parents you were an art prodigy. Your mother begged William to enroll you in private lessons, but he stubbornly refused. Said you were going to spend your life at the bank and that was that."

Groaning, wishing like hell Alice would leave him alone, Dalton said, "What does any of this have to do with the here and now? In three days, my future's set in stone. Just the way I like it."

"Did you break up with that beauty?"

"Heck, yes." He bolted upright. "Isn't that what all you overbearing snoops wanted me to do?"

"Oh, Dalton…" She shook her head.

"What?" Fiddling with a dandelion, he wished he'd stayed at the office.

"Does this have anything to do with Carly?"

"No."

"You think because Carly was an artist and Rose is a dancer, that they're two peas in a pod?" When he didn't answer, she nudged his shoulder.

"Absolutely not."

"Then what's the problem?"

"At the moment, you."

Sighing, she pushed to her feet. "You might be all grown-up on the outside, but on the inside, you've still got an awful lot of maturing to do."

IF THERE WAS ONE THING Dalton hated worse than banking, it was being lectured, then realizing it was time for him to admit his mistakes. It was that very realization that had led him to his current location. The head of Duffy's Barbecue's back-room conference table.

Dalton clinked his water glass with his butter knife and cleared his throat to get everyone's attention. "Thank you all for agreeing to meet on such short notice. I've had an issue crop up that I believe is going to take all of us to fix."

Frank raised his hand.

"Yes?"

"Can we order first? I'm starving."

By a unanimous vote—aside from Dalton's—the Hot

Pepper chamber of commerce's executive board elected to eat first, deal with his trauma later.

"That's better," Frank said thirty minutes later, pushing his plate away. "Now, what seems to be the problem?"

Dalton said, "How many of you have seen me around town with a certain dance instructor?"

All eleven shot up their hands.

"How many thought we seemed like a good match?"

All present concurred.

"You do seem awfully taken with her," Mona said. "I never expected you to learn to tango quite that well, but then, looks like you might've had a few private lessons."

Frank and a couple of the other guys backslapped each other while howling with laughter.

"Okay, simmer down." Dalton slammed Alice's gavel. "Making a long story short, I screwed up royally. I won't bore you with the details, but suffice to say that I was wrong. I love Rose and her daughter very much."

"Aw…" Mona said, hands clasped in front of her on the table. "I always did think you two looked cute together. And clearly, her little girl adores you. You're a perfect match. I vote we should take it upon ourselves to get them back together."

"Why else do you think I agreed to take this meeting?" Alice asked, her voice all huffy, with her hands on her hips. "I swear, Mona, do you just wake up in the morning, planning to steal my thunder?"

Lips pursed, Mona shot Alice her fiercest glare.

"All right, then," Dalton said, again slamming the

gavel to counteract the chatter. "By another show of hands, who wants to enact an emergency matchmaker plan in order to save me, Rose and Anna?"

Everyone present raised his or her hand, save for one. Alice.

"You have a problem?" he inquired.

She blurted out, "One thing has crossed my mind."

"Shoot."

Taking a moment before answering, in typical Alice fashion, she drew out the drama. "What about what you and I discussed in the park? What all of a sudden changed your mind? Was it, by chance, anything I said?"

Holding back a growl, Dalton admitted, "Yes, Alice. You told me to grow up, and by the time we've enacted our plan, I'm hoping that's exactly what I'll have done."

Chapter Sixteen

"Wow, Dad," Dalton said over the jazz band at Saturday night's party. "You look amazing for a guy who just had heart surgery." As opposed to Dalton, who felt like the walking dead after having suffered a sleepless night wondering if his plan would work or blow up in his face.

"I feel amazing. According to the doc, half my blood wasn't making it around. Is it any wonder I nearly croaked?"

"Stop," Dalton's mom said. "You were no more near croaking than the bronze bullfrog in our garden pond."

Though his mom's words were light, Dalton didn't miss the worry in her eyes, or the way her hands never left his father's arm. He and Rose could have been like that after decades of marriage. He missed her with a biting clarity. And he realized what an idiot he'd been to give her up. His plan had to work.

"Carol!" his mom called to one of her friends. "Wait right there. I need to ask you a decorating question." To her son, she said, "Watch the rich food tonight. Joan said your heartburn's been acting up." Towing his dad along with her, his mother worked the room, leaving Dalton on his own with his worries.

A waiter passed.

Dalton snatched a glass bubbling with champagne from the man's silver tray. Fighting the urge to down it in one swallow, he took a few sips before hitting the hors d'oeuvre table.

His mom had gone all-out on the party, which made him feel worse for being so uptight.

Tall, tapered candles in crystal holders were everywhere and hundreds of white roses had the air smelling heavy and sweet. Couples danced to the jazz band, and he wished Rose were here so he could take her in his arms and show what a good student he was. As badly as he'd behaved, she'd no doubt never speak to him again. And really, could he blame her? He'd been a fool for allowing a mistake from his past to quite possibly destroy a brilliant future.

Alice danced alongside him, champagne in one hand, a mini spinach quiche in the other. "How're you doin' there, stud? You're pale."

"Could you *please* leave me alone? Dad's about to make his announcement, and I've got a lot on my mind."

"Someone got up on the wrong side of the bed. What's got you so cranky?"

"Nothing, all right? I'm just not in the mood for partying—at least not until I see if Rose and Anna show up."

Alice blessedly sashayed off to pester someone else while Dalton got another drink. He'd taken a few sips when the band stopped, and his dad ambled onto the stage, taking the mic.

"Test, test," he said, tapping the sensitive tip and causing a squelch of feedback that had everyone wincing. "Oops." He grinned. "Guess I don't know my own strength."

The audience politely tittered.

"As most of you know, tonight is special. It marks the closing of some chapters, and the opening of others." He cleared his throat. Dabbed the corners of his eyes with a white handkerchief.

Seeing his father choked up like this made Dalton feel a thousand times worse. He hated the fact that a big portion of his plan would quite possibly cause his father pain. But, with Alice's speech still ringing in his head, he realized this bold step was something he should've done years earlier.

"I could bore you all to tears with a lifetime of reminiscing, but what I'd rather do is get straight to the point. After fifty years spent in one capacity or another at the First National Bank of Hot Pepper, I'm officially stepping down."

While the audience roared with applause, Dalton's pulse thundered.

His portion of the night fast approached.

The mere thought made him feel ill.

He wanted so badly to be with Rose right now, and

Anna. Whether they were watching TV or washing dishes or messing with Play-Doh, he just wanted to be with them, to experience that sense of being a family again.

Were they here? *Please, God, let them be here.*

"Thank you, thank you," his father said. "Now, everyone simmer down, as the best part of the evening's still to come. The part where I name my successor. This person is not only personable, but sharp as a tack. Partially under their guidance, the bank has reached proportions my father and grandfather never would've believed possible. Under this person's continued leadership, I have nothing but the highest expectations for our institution to keep growing, and keep making our customers proud that they bank with us. So now, without further ado, may I proudly present your new president—"

Dalton stood. Pasted on a smile. Marched up to the stage and took the mic. "—Alice Craigmoore."

Gasps.

Whispers.

And then applause, applause, applause.

Dalton glanced behind him to his shocked parents, murmuring for their ears only, "Sorry, Dad. But I can't keep living a lie. Of course, if anyone at the bank ever needs me, I don't mind pitching in every once in a while, but I just can't do it day after day. I want to pursue my sculpting." *See if I can make a living with my hands instead of this mush in my head that used to be my brains.* "Alice, on the other hand, isn't only highly qualified for the job, but very much wants it. In my professional opinion, she'll be the perfect fit."

"Son," his father said with a surprisingly cordial pat to his back, "I'm proud of you. I'd be lying if I said I wasn't disappointed, but it took a lot of balls to come up here and turn down this job."

"Thanks, Dad." Dalton swallowed what felt like a rock in his throat. "Coming from you, that means a lot." More like everything.

His father and mother embraced Alice in teary hugs. Alice also seemed choked up, but overall smiling and looking at least a foot taller.

"Thank you for that lovely applause," Alice said into the mic. "I feel reasonably sure I know each and every one of you, and I can honestly say that outside of my wedding day and the births of my three children, I've never had a prouder moment. I've been with the bank for more years than I can count. My coworkers, and our founding family, the Montgomerys, mean the world to me. I will do my utmost to perform with the loyalty and integrity that they've shown in choosing me for the job."

More applause filled the room, this time louder, and definitely heartfelt.

Though Dalton still reeled from the most pleasant shock of having his dad so easily digest his news, he found himself genuinely happy for Alice. No one deserved it more.

Kind of like the way he deserved for Rose and Anna to have refused his invitation. He'd planned to wow

Rose with his announcement, then woo her into the night with dancing and champagne and dozens of sincere apologies he'd prayed might convince her to take him back.

How did he know he loved her? The same way he knew to breathe. She and Carly were nothing alike. He'd been insulting Rose to have even for a moment suggested they were.

Alice was back at the mic. "William mentioned that tonight's a night for looking forward, not back. And in that spirit, my first official announcement is that effective immediately, for those of you not privy to our previous onstage whisperings, our current VP, Dalton Montgomery, will be taking an indefinite leave of absence. Should he care to return, his office will always be available, but I have something here I think he'd much rather do." She waved what looked like three thick travel agency portfolios.

Huh?

What was Alice doing? This wasn't part of the plan.

"In these packets are tickets for an art tour of Europe. For those of you who don't already know, Dalton isn't only good at facts and figures, but also sculpting. According to a couple of girls I recently had the pleasure of getting to know better, he's also become quite a good significant other and father. So…in that spirit, here are Rose and Anna Vasquez, who have a question to ask our Dalton."

Knees rubbery, Dalton felt ready to collapse, but keeping his eyes on his two beautiful girls, he managed to stay strong despite the lump forming at the back of his throat. No wonder his dad had taken the news so well. He'd been given advance notice.

Anna took the mic. "Mr. Dalton? If you're out there, would you please marry us? I *really* wanna go on vacation."

"Anna!" Rose, looking drop-dead gorgeous in a red satin dress, accidentally scolded for all to hear.

All present roared with laughter and applause.

"Sorry, Mr. Dalton. I was s'posed to say we love you, but I do wanna go on vacation. Oh—and I want you to be my new dad, too."

Striding through the crowd, Dalton found his way back onstage. He kissed Rose full on the lips, then bent down and gave Anna a bear hug. In Rose's ear, he whispered, "I don't know how you managed to turn my own surprise upside down, but you have to know I'm sorry, and that I love you so much. I was crazy to have ever doubted you—us. In fact, I—"

"Oh, stop. *Mi novio,* I had a sneaking suspicion you'd come back to me. It was only a matter of time."

"Too much time," he said on the heels of a moan, kissing her again. "If I haven't mentioned it lately, I love you."

"Is that a yes to our proposal?" she asked, brown eyes shimmering.

"Not just yes," he growled for her ears only, lifting her, hugging her, spinning her around. "But hell yes."

"What about me?" Anna asked, jumping beside him in a shimmering hot-pink dress.

"Of course I love you, too."

As a Congratulations Anna, Rose and Dalton banner dropped from the ceiling, so did white confetti and silver balloons.

Hugging his girls close, Dalton happened to glance past Rose's shoulder to his mom and dad.

Grinning, crying, they held each other, clapping along with the rest of the crowd for all they were worth.

The weight lifted from Dalton's shoulders was immense. As was the depth of his love.

From the contented looks in their eyes, he'd been the only one present not in on the fact that Alice had double-crossed him in a wonderful way. True to Alice's nature, she'd planned and schemed behind his back. And he adored her for it!

Later, while the band played on and the impromptu engagement party wound down, Anna sound asleep on his mother's fur coat, Dalton tugged Rose into a private corner and kissed her hungrily. "Do you have any idea how much I missed you?"

"Considering I missed you even more, yes."

"Mind my asking how you pulled this off?"

"With the help of my fellow chamber members, it wasn't a big deal."

"Right," he said with a chuckle. "Who talked to my dad?"

"Oddly enough, he came to Alice. Apparently, during your talks at the hospital, you weren't quite as convincing as you thought."

"*Great.* He's not on the verge of keeling over, is he?"

"Does he look like it?"

He glanced where Rose pointed. His parents embraced on the dance floor, barely moving, but clearly enjoying the evening.

"See?" Rose teased. "They're happy. We're happy. Relax."

"I'm not sure I know how."

"I'll teach you."

"Hot Pepper Dance Academy offers relaxation lessons?"

"We'll start."

When Dalton met Rose's heated glance, she knew without him saying a word he wanted to tango. Slipping her hand in his, she accompanied him to an empty spot on the crowded floor.

Her cheek against his solid chest, she smiled, content in the knowledge that once again dance had worked magic. Changed lives. Dalton's, his parents', Alice's, and least expected of all, but most welcome, her daughter's and her own.

* * * * *

For a sneak preview of Marie Ferrarella's
DOCTOR IN THE HOUSE,
coming to NEXT in September,
please turn the page.

He didn't look like an unholy terror.

But maybe that reputation was exaggerated, Bailey DelMonico thought as she turned in her chair to look toward the doorway.

The man didn't seem scary at all.

Dr. Munro, or Ivan the Terrible, was tall, with an athletic build and wide shoulders. The cheekbones beneath what she estimated to be day-old stubble were prominent. His hair was light brown and just this side of unruly. Munro's hair looked as if he used his fingers for a comb and didn't care who knew it.

The eyes were brown, almost black as they were aimed at her. There was no other word for it. Aimed. As if he were debating whether or not to fire at point-blank range.

Somewhere in the back of her mind, a line from a B movie, "Be afraid—be very afraid…" whispered along the perimeter of her brain. Warning her. Almost against her will, it caused her to brace her shoulders. Bailey had to remind herself to breathe in and out like a normal person.

The chief of staff, Dr. Bennett, had tried his level best

to put her at ease and had almost succeeded. But an air of tension had entered with Munro. She wondered if Dr. Bennett was bracing himself, as well, bracing for some kind of disaster or explosion.

"Ah, here he is now," Harold Bennett announced needlessly. The smile on his lips was slightly forced, and the look in his gray, kindly eyes held a warning as he looked at his chief neurosurgeon. "We were just talking about you, Dr. Munro."

"Can't imagine why," Ivan replied dryly.

Harold cleared his throat, as if that would cover the less than friendly tone of voice Ivan had just displayed. "Dr. Munro, this is the young woman I was telling you about yesterday."

Now his eyes dissected her. Bailey felt as if she were undergoing a scalpel-less autopsy right then and there. "Ah yes, the Stanford Special."

He made her sound like something that was listed at the top of a third-rate diner menu. There was enough contempt in his voice to offend an entire delegation from the UN.

Summoning the bravado that her parents always claimed had been infused in her since the moment she first drew breath, Bailey put out her hand. "Hello. I'm Dr. Bailey DelMonico."

Ivan made no effort to take the hand offered to him. Instead, he slid his long, lanky form bonelessly into the chair beside her. He proceeded to move the chair ever so slightly so that there was even more space between them. Ivan faced the chief of staff, but the words he spoke were addressed to her.

"You're a doctor, DelMonico, when I say you're a doctor," he informed her coldly, sparing her only one frosty glance to punctuate the end of his statement.

Harold stifled a sigh. "Dr. Munro is going to take over your education. Dr. Munro—" he fixed Ivan with a steely gaze that had been known to send lesser doctors running for their antacids, but, as always, seemed to have no effect on the chief neurosurgeon "—I want you to award her every consideration. From now on, Dr. DelMonico is to be your shadow, your sponge and your assistant." He emphasized the last word as his eyes locked with Ivan's. "Do I make myself clear?"

For his part, Ivan seemed completely unfazed. He merely nodded, his eyes and expression unreadable. "Perfectly."

His hand was on the doorknob. Bailey sprang to her feet. Her chair made a scraping noise as she moved it back and then quickly joined the neurosurgeon before he could leave the office.

Closing the door behind him, Ivan leaned over and whispered into her ear, "Just so you know, I'm going to be your worst nightmare."

Ria Sterling has the gift—or is it a curse?—of seeing a person's future in his or her photograph. Unfortunately, when detective Carrick Jones brings her a missing person's case, she glimpses his partner's ID—and sees imminent murder. And when her vision comes true, Ria becomes the prime suspect. Carrick isn't convinced this beautiful woman committed the crime...but does he believe she has the special powers to solve it?

Look for

Seeing Is Believing

by

Kate Austin

**Available October
wherever you buy books.**

HN88144

REQUEST YOUR FREE BOOKS!
2 FREE NOVELS PLUS 2
FREE GIFTS!

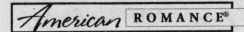

Heart, Home & Happiness!

HAR07

® HARLEQUIN®

Mediterranean
NIGHTS™

*Sail aboard the luxurious Alexandra's Dream and
experience glamour, romance, mystery and revenge!*

Coming in October 2007...

AN AFFAIR TO
REMEMBER

by
Karen Kendall

When Captain Nikolas Pappas first fell in love with
Helena Stamos, he was a penniless deckhand and she
was the daughter of a shipping magnate. But he's
never forgiven himself for the way he left her—and
fifteen years later, he's determined to win her back.

Though the attraction is still there, Helena is hesitant
to get involved. Nick left her once...what's to stop
him from doing it again?

HM38964

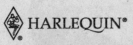

HARLEQUIN®

American ROMANCE®

COMING NEXT MONTH

#1181 THE RANCHER'S FAMILY THANKSGIVING
by Cathy Gillen Thacker
Texas Legacies: The Carrigans
Susie Carrigan and Tyler McCabe have always been friends—and sometimes lovers. Both fiercely independent, they've never been a couple, and never sought marriage. To anyone. But once Susie's matchmaking parents start setting her up on dates, Tyler starts thinking about their "friendship" differently. And wants those other guys to stay away from "his girl"!

#1182 MARRIAGE ON HER MIND by Cindi Myers
With a failed wedding behind her, Casey Jernigan arrives in eccentric Crested Butte, Colorado, ready for single life. But her landlord, Max Overbridge, could challenge that decision. His easygoing charm and his obvious interest are making her reconsider those wedding bells!

#1183 THE GOOD MOTHER by Shelley Galloway
Motherhood
Evie Ray and August Meyer were once high-school sweethearts. Now Evie's a single mom, doing her best to juggle work and motherhood, while August has taken over his parents' vacation resort. Seeing each other again, they realize there are still sparks between them. But will they be able to overcome past hurts to find love again?

#1184 FOR THE CHILDREN by Marin Thomas
Hearts of Appalachia
Self-reliant schoolteacher Jo Macpherson is on a mission to instill pride in the children of a Scotch-Irish clan living in Heather's Hollow, in Appalachia. She never expected to have to deal with intrepid Sullivan Mooreland, a far too appealing newspaperman who's on a mission to track down information about the Hollow that Jo has vowed not to reveal.

www.eHarlequin.com

HARCNM0907